Former special ops soldier Treb Carson has returned to his ranching roots joining up with the New Horizon Ranch. Afghanistan and the loss of his brother have him ready to move forward into happier times–he's looking for love and to start a family. He's not expecting to be captivated by Megan Tanner, the completely wrong woman for his plans. The workaholic, new veterinarian in town doesn't have marriage on her agenda and she's made that clear, but he can't get her or the kiss they share off his mind.

Megan Tanner has her personal reasons for not believing in happily-ever-after, but now she's moved to the hometown of the Matchmakin' Posse of Mule Hollow. Avoiding their antics is easy for now, it's calving season and that means no time for anything but work and building her vet practice. But then she's blindsided by the smokin'-hot, ex-military cowboy and the immediate sparks she can't deny or the kiss she can't forget.

Treb knows all the reasons why Megan isn't the woman for him...but he can't seem to stop himself. Now he's determined to find out why Megan is so against falling in love and proving to her that she can trust him with her heart.

And he's got a certain three nosey ladies on his side...can the "Posse" help this couple find their happily-ever-after?

# TREB

New Horizon Ranch, Book Six

# DEBRA
# CLOPTON

*Treb*

Copyright © 2016 Debra Clopton Parks

# CHAPTER ONE

"**M**om, stop."

"Megan Renee Tanner," her mother enunciated precisely. "I will not stop. This is the third night in a row that I've called you to find out you are spending time with the cows. Not a man. You're a young woman, but you aren't getting any younger and all your evenings shouldn't be spent with cattle. Or horses, dogs, goats, or cats for that matter. You need to be spending time with a man every once in a while or you'll become a cat lady...or—or a *cow* lady, heaven forbid."

Her mother had her on that. It was the third night on the job where she'd gotten in closer to sunrise than sunset. "I'm not having this conversation right now, Mom."

Megan transferred the phone to her other ear and held it in place with her shoulder as she lifted the tail of the high-risk show cow. It was about to give birth at any moment but so far so good. She just hoped she'd gotten the baby turned and there would be no more complications. Her arm and shoulder ached from having wrestled the calf into place and she was three days sleep-deprived. All of which she wasn't about to admit to her mother.

"You won't have the conversation about your love life because you know as well as I do that it doesn't exist. At this very moment, you're probably in the middle of pulling a calf or worse, have your arm shoved up—"

"Mom, come on. Let it go."

"I won't. You need to stop working those ridiculous hours and get a life. A love life. You're not getting any younger and the longer you wait, the harder it'll be. Your sisters didn't wait so long…"

"Right. And look what it got them."

"That's not nice. They were happy while they were married."

"*While* being the pivotal word here. Now they're each involved in their own World War Three divorce nightmare." Both of her sisters had married men who had decided monogamy was not for them. Bad judgment seemed to run in the family…and now both sisters were devastated because of it. It had been right in front of them all along, considering their mother had gone through the trauma of divorce three times.

*Three* and had recently married number four. Her mom trying to sell Megan on the merits of matrimonial bliss fell way short. Megan would take the south end of a birthing cow any day to the heartache and drama that came when a marriage fell apart.

"Honey, you need to be more positive. Love is a beautiful thing."

And that was her mom. Ever the optimist when it came to believing in happily-ever-afters. She devoured romance books and was a sap for romantic movies.

Her judgment on how the world *really* worked was way off the charts.

"It doesn't last and you know it." Megan had seen the real world from the sidelines of both sisters and her mom…and she'd hardened her heart to all of it.

"When the right one comes along, it does."

"Mom, please. I need to go. This cow is about to—"

"I knew it! You *are* midwifing a heifer. Megan, you once believed in fairy tales. You loved Prince Charming."

Megan closed her eyes and counted to ten. "Mom, I was a kid. I grew up. Oops, I see a hoof—not good. I've got to go."

She hung up and groaned—both from the conversation she'd had with her mother and the fact that despite all her work on turning the calf, it was still coming out the hard way. It was going to be a rough night. But then, there was one thing her mother had never understood about Megan's career choice. She loved it. Loved everything about helping animals and being a veterinarian. She even liked the late nights…they kept her busy and that was just like she wanted it.

The sun rose in faint hues of pink and pale blue as Treb Carson rode his stallion across the open pasture toward the misty sunrise. His thoughts were troubled—he'd had another sleepless night where the dreams woke him…explosions, shouting, and the endless sound of gunfire.

It was over a year since he'd come home but he'd come to believe he'd never get the sound of war out of his mind. He'd learned there was no chance of sleep once the dreams started and he'd found riding in open country usually helped remind him that he was here, alive and blessed.

The smooth, soothing feel of the horse beneath him, the fresh air…the peaceful serenity of the morning calmed his soul…but not this morning.

He reached the peak of the hill and pulled his horse to a halt. Resting a wrist on the saddle horn, he watched the morning come quietly over the hill. The sunrise always gave him hope…promise of a new day, a new beginning.

Today it was time to move forward, to move on with his life.

He breathed in the cool, early morning air, and continued to mull over his thoughts as the sunrise broke through the mist, gaining strength and vibrancy as it rose. He thanked God that, unlike his brother and countless others who'd given the ultimate sacrifice for their country, he'd come home alive. And now it was time to draw a line in the dirt and step across it.

Despite the lingering nightmares, it was time to make the choice to move from just existing since coming home and to start living.

His brother would want it. And as much as he wished it had been him and not Mark who had perished, that wasn't the way it was.

Treb straightened in the saddle as he made up his mind. With determination in his heart, he turned his horse around and headed back toward his home for now—the bunkhouse cabin the ranch offered its wranglers.

He decided it was time to look for a place of his own.

He enjoyed his work at the New Horizon Ranch. He liked the partners who owned the place and enjoyed this area. Mule Hollow was great cattle country and the people were amazing.

So it was time to settle down and there was no other place he'd rather do that than Mule Hollow, Texas.

His attention was suddenly caught by a large area of churned-up pasture. A sure signal that a destructive group of wild hogs had begun an attack on this area. Changing route, he followed the prints toward the woods until he saw more destroyed pastureland. They were definitely on a rip and tear path, headed toward the creek. Treb reached the water's edge and followed it until he reached the fence line that ran along the access road. The fence stopped his progress as the creek continued on under the small bridge of the road and on into the ranch's land on the other side. Prints in the mud showed that the hogs had traveled along this route.

He'd have to bring a crew out and set up cage traps to catch them and move them off the ranch.

Wild hogs bred fast and multiplied in the blink of an eye, costing ranchers massive amounts of revenue. He'd need to get on this quick. Turning back, he started toward the ranch compound when he spotted a blue truck he didn't recognize down the road under a stand of trees on the other side of the fence.

Altering his path again, he went to check it out. As he drew near, he could see a pair of cowboy boots propped up on the dash and a cowboy slumped in the seat, his head leaned back with a hat pulled down over his eyes. Probably sleeping off a night of drinking. Treb could remember a time in his early days when that might have been him. He'd come a long way since those years of rebellious living.

The truck was pulled close enough to the pipe fence that he didn't bother to dismount. Instead, he stretched over the pipe and rapped his knuckles on the half rolled-down window.

A hand came up and slowly lifted the hat a fraction. Treb stared into the wide, tired eyes of a woman. Rich amber eyes that he could imagine would shimmer in sunlight.

She yanked her booted feet to the floorboard with a bang and sat up so fast her hat fell off her head, revealing strands of caramel-colored hair that had escaped from a loose ponytail. He swallowed a lump that had formed in his throat and just stared at the beautiful, sleep-mushed female. He'd been prepared to greet a hungover cowboy, not a gorgeous woman.

"Um..." his voice faltered—*That never happened.* He tried again. "Mornin', ma'am," he drawled and tapped the front edge of his hat in greeting.

Despite her knee-jerk reaction when he'd first arrived, she was dazed too. She blinked hard and looked from him to her surroundings with sleep-dazed eyes. "Morning to you too. I guess I slept later than I thought I would."

It was clear by her words that she'd deemed him a non-threat. "I reckon." He nodded toward her and her truck. "But only if you normally lounge in bed till dawn."

"Luckily, I don't normally have to sleep in my

truck." Her honey-toned eyes lit up. "Though, there was a time during vet school while in between jobs that I had to...never mind, that's a long story and you're a stranger, so I think I'll cut it off there."

She smiled and Treb felt a sharp jab of attraction. "Fair enough. But do you mind enlightening me on why you're on the New Horizon Ranch property?"

She hid a yawn and her light-brown brows crinkled as she glanced down the road and then back at him. "I just pulled onto the nearest side road. Didn't know I was trespassing. I was coming back late from trying to save a mother cow and newborn calf, and I nearly went to sleep at the wheel. I opted to pull over here to just close my eyes for a few moments. Obviously I forgot to set an alarm."

"You're a veterinarian?" The information clicked into place. He glanced at the truck, with its side panels that could house meds and equipment she might need. He hadn't paid attention to that until now.

"I am."

"And you pulled over into the trees and rolled your window down and went to sleep—that's a pretty careless thing to do. Do you realize you could have been hurt?" He couldn't believe she was an intelligent woman and had acted so carelessly.

Irritation flashed in her eyes. Then she slowly lifted her other hand—the one that she'd kept below eye level on the other side of the door until now. A Glock firearm was held securely in her grip. "I can take care of myself."

If he wanted to, he could have that stupid gun away from her before she could blink her pretty eyes, but he didn't point that out. "So, I assume you know how to use that?"

"I do." Her eyes narrowed. "And I'm not in the least bit afraid to use it. My war vet granddaddy believed in making all his granddaughters expert marksman. Believe me, no one is going to mess with me."

"I'll point out that you were sleeping harder than a bear in hibernation when I rapped on your half-opened window. I could have had an arm through that open glass before you had one eye open."

She cocked her head and studied him. "And I'd

have shot you."

"More likely you'd have shot off your toe or something when I startled you."

"Maybe. But *then* I'd have shot you." She stared at him in challenge.

His brows dipped and he was at a loss for words that she would put herself into such a vulnerable situation. He'd seen far too much in his combat tour to make any kind of sense of someone just acting downright senseless.

"All I can say is I hope this isn't common practice for you and I'd appreciate it if you'd put that thing away for now. I'm not here to hurt you. I work on the ranch."

She held his gaze for a long moment then slowly lowered the gun. "Sorry, but a girl can't be too careful."

"Careful? Honey, you were careless."

Fire flashed again. "I guess you can have your own opinion. Look, I need a cup of coffee." She cocked her head out the window, staring hard at his horse. "You wouldn't happen to have a hot cup of coffee in there, would you?"

He realized she'd zeroed in on the thermos that stuck out of his saddlebag. She opened her truck door and got out and he found himself at a loss for words again as his gaze drifted down her long legs and shapely figure. She wore a simple T-shirt and jeans that hugged her curves. The jeans were tucked into well-worn boots. She looked every inch the cowgirl vet that she was. And as spunky as she'd appeared so far.

She grabbed the top rail of the pipe fence that separated them, then lifted her face to him. He just stared down at her, taking in her small splattering of freckles and clear skin.

"Is there anything in it?" she asked again, prompting him when he hadn't answered her.

He yanked his thoughts off her attributes. "I do, as a matter of fact."

"Would you consider sharing it with me? I need to get back home and shower before I start my daily rounds and coffee right now would be heaven sent. I'm truly grateful that you showed up and woke me or I would have been late for work."

Treb found himself grinning at the anticipatory way she was eyeing his thermos of coffee. Obviously coffee had the power to erase any displeasure she'd had with him.

"Glad I could help," he drawled and tried not to get lost in those eyes. Instead, he tugged the thermos from his saddlebag and unscrewed the attached cup.

"Hold on," she snapped. She spun back to her truck, leaned inside and a moment later, she whirled back to him, holding a paper cup up triumphantly. "Bingo! Coffee to go."

She popped the lid off and poured out the few drops of leftover coffee. "My lone cup from last night—it's been far too long ago." She held it up to him and smiled.

Treb stared down at her. That engaging smile, those now sparkling eyes…he could only imagine how they'd sparkle when she wasn't worn out.

"A-hem." She cleared her throat dramatically and wiggled the cup, drawing his attention to the fact that he'd been staring and not pouring.

Too quickly, he reached for the cup and his fingers

wrapped completely around hers. A kick-in-the-stomach-from-a-bucking-bull slam of electrical attraction raced up his arm, jarring him with its impact. What was up with him? He hadn't reacted like this to a woman in…well, in ever.

Her eyes widened and flashed with instant energy, making him almost positive she'd felt it too. She slipped her fingers out of his and focused on the coffee. "It smells fabulous."

He poured the coffee. "Here you go. That should clear your mind." He placed it into her hands. Steam curled from the cup and she was very careful taking it from him. He didn't miss that she was also very careful to avoid contact with him again.

Just as he was careful not to touch her either.

"Heavenly." She breathed in the scent of the coffee and then pursed her lips and took a sip.

His gut tightened as he watched her and was startled when hot coffee spilled on his thigh. "Hot," he bit out and yanked his gaze from watching her to concentrate on pouring himself a cup.

"Careful," she warned. "This is amazingly hot.

That's a great thermos. You'll have to tell me what brand so I can get myself one. It could come in handy on lone, late-night calls." She took another sip. "Thanks so much. I've got to go. My dog, Archie, is probably wondering what happened to me."

She took another long sip, smiled charmingly at him.

He just stared down at her, frozen in place as she turned and climbed back into her truck...*Archie was one lucky dog.*

"Drive safe," he called.

She lifted the cup in salute. "Duty calls." She cranked her truck and shifted it into gear.

Treb sipped his coffee, trying to appear unaffected, as he watched her make a wide U-turn and head back down the access road, disappearing in a cloud of dust.

He almost thought he'd dreamed her. That the escapade actually hadn't happened.

But he knew even in his crazy dreams that he'd never have dreamed up this woman. He realized then that he didn't even know her name. And she didn't know his.

But he would.

She had been interesting, though a little soft in the head if she believed she was safe out here. There were crazies in this world, even in small towns. Common sense was something that everyone needed to use and gun-toting-vet-lady hadn't shown she had any to use.

New Horizon Ranch did a lot of business with the vet clinic. He hoped they didn't have any of their champion stock that needed looking after while Susan Turner was on maternity leave. He'd have to mention this to the owners of the ranch. And after that, it wasn't any of his concern. Not until he had his own herd. Then he'd have reasons to be concerned about whether he wanted her working on his animals. Until then, it was someone else's call.

He poured out his coffee and twisted the lid onto the thermos, still very aware of the way he'd reacted to her touch. And very aware that he wouldn't be acting on that attraction.

A woman who worked all hours of the day and night and sometimes slept in her truck was not the type of woman he had an interest in—even if he was attracted to her.

He was almost back to the ranch compound before it dawned on him that he hadn't thought about his past or bad dream since she'd pulled her hat off her head and turned those eyes of hers on him.

# CHAPTER TWO

*H*oly *barn-burner—that had been one hot cowboy.*

He'd been a little maddening, and somewhat condescending, but she had to remember that the man was a cowboy…and obviously his protective instincts had come out.

And she *had* left the window down. Not exactly her smartest move ever.

Megan thought about Hot Cowboy all the way back home—realizing quickly that she hadn't asked his name. But Hot Cowboy worked.

Archie waited for her on the front porch, tail thumping. His smile brightened her day like none other. She slammed her truck door, hurried up the walk and engulfed him in a hug. He let out a big woof of approval and rested his large blond head on her shoulder in a doggie hug.

"Did you miss me, big boy? Looks like you did a good job protecting the place for me."

He wiggled and woofed as he pranced in a circle, displaying his alpha protector side.

He was a marshmallow but took his job seriously in her absence.

"Okay, big boy, let's go feed the menagerie." She had goats, including her old Daisy Lou that she'd had for fifteen years and a milk cow named Buttercup. She gave everyone an affectionate scrub along their necks, put out their feed and then jogged back to the house and started a pot of coffee brewing before she jumped in the shower. Hectic was not a strong enough word for what she'd gotten herself into when she'd taken this job. Her only saving grace was that Susan was coming back part-time in three weeks. She and her baby were home and doing great. Megan was thrilled for them, but she'd been at this job for four weeks and she was worn out.

Yes, she loved to work, but this was a little nuts.

Showered and changed, she grabbed a cup of coffee and took a second to lean against the counter and enjoy a very small moment of calmness. Archie watched her with his head tilted.

"Don't look at me like that. Life is going to calm down. Calving season is very nearly done and we have survived."

He barked and thumped his tail on the hardwood floor.

"Fine, you're right. We've barely survived. I can't believe I had to stop on the side of the road and sleep in my truck."

Her mother would absolutely have a cow herself if she knew Megan had done this. But it couldn't be helped. Megan had gone to sleep at the wheel and nearly hit a tree and that was that. She'd pulled off the road—a little delirious, she'd been so sleepy—and had just planned an hour...which would have been four a.m. The last thing she'd expected after she tugged her Glock from under the seat had been to be awakened by a hunky dude on a horse at dawn.

Megan's thoughts went right back to the cowboy and a shiver raced through her. *He had been something.* As if sensing she'd gotten lost in thought, Archie whined.

"Sorry, buddy, but I can't take your accusing eyes any longer. I've got to run." She gave Archie another quick hug and then refilled her insulated mug before she led him back outside. Back on the road a few moments later, her mind mulled over her situation.

She had been told before she took this job that it was hard for one person to keep up with. Susan had done it for about three years and had told her that if she liked the work that she was going to be more than ready to either hire someone on permanently or acquire a partner in the business. With a new baby, she knew there was no way she could attempt to take care of all the ranches around Mule Hollow alone.

Megan was considering it. But last night had been a long night and the night before that had been a long one too. And the night before that. And so on. She was going to have to get some sleep soon or she wouldn't live long enough to consider taking the position. Sleeping on the side of the road wasn't something she did unless it was absolutely necessary. And last night, it had been obvious she was desperate or she wouldn't have forgotten to roll up her window. Wouldn't have forgotten to set her alarm. The fact that she'd pulled her gun from beneath the seat where she always kept it when she was working alone would have made her granddaddy proud.

But the truth was she'd basically pulled the truck over and passed out.

She hadn't been about to tell the cowboy that bit of info. Not when he'd already been looking at her as though she had two heads, two very dumb heads, on her shoulders because she'd left her window down.

Nope, he would never know that she had done that by accident. She'd look even more incompetent if she admitted that she'd run herself so long she'd almost shut down before she got the truck stopped.

As far as the cowboy was concerned, she would

maintain that she was a self-assured, gun-toting woman with no fears.

She almost laughed at that but she didn't. She'd love to be that person. And maybe one day she would be. Right now, she just had to make it through one more day and then the weekend relief doctor would arrive to take over for those few days. If it wasn't for him she wouldn't have survived this last month.

She'd make good use of the one night of blessed sleep. She just had to make it through tonight. And she'd prefer not to have to sleep in the truck again.

"Well, good morning," Betty, the receptionist, said a few minutes later when Megan walked through the back door. She slapped a stack of patient folders on the desk. "Hope you have your jogging shoes on this morning because you're going to need it. You look like leftovers this morning. Bad night?"

"Oh yeah. But all is well. I saw the parking lot is full. What's up?"

"I'm telling you that phone started ringing the moment I walked through the door and it hasn't stopped. The moon always brings them out."

Megan laughed. "Is that what it is? Well, keep the coffee brewing. I have a feeling I'm going to need it."

"I will and I'll pick up lunch from Sam's Diner so you'll get something decent in your stomach. You look like you didn't get any sleep last night. And I know you probably haven't taken time to eat."

Betty was a mother hen. She took her job seriously and tried to make sure Megan got something to eat, at least for lunch. "How did you get to know me so well in so short a time?"

She laughed. "You're just like Susan. Out to save every creature you can and going to die trying. Sheesh, you girls aren't going to be young forever. You've got to take time for nutrition at least. Thankfully this baby is nipping Susan's death wish in the bud. Maybe marriage, home, and family is what you need to get some perspective. Life isn't all about work."

"I don't have a death wish. I just want to do a good job."

"You are. You are. Now eat this and I'll bring in the first patient." She slammed a nutrition bar on the desk and hiked a brow. "And don't even think about not eating that."

"Thanks, Mom." Megan peeled the wrapper and took a bite as Betty hustled out.

And so her day went into overdrive as she saw pups and cats and even goats—she loved goats. Cute, little ugly rascals just made her laugh. Later, some horses were brought in and even a pet hedgehog, which added a few prickles to the day. However, by four, the place was cleared out and Megan collapsed into her chair for a few minutes. How Susan had managed by herself for three years was beyond her.

Betty came into the room. "I hate to tell you this but you've got an emergency out at New Horizon Ranch with one of their prized heifers."

Megan immediately recognized that this was the ranch she'd been on that morning. Her pulse instantly revved up at the thought of seeing Hot Cowboy again.

Her mother would be so happy.

"Do you feel okay?" Betty paused the briefing she was giving about the emergency.

"I'm fine. Why?"

"You're flushed. Do you have a fever? Your

cheeks are pinker than Heavenly Inspirations Hair Salon in town."

*That was pink.* That two-story tall wooden building was hot pink and stood out like a beacon for miles away. Megan's hand went to her cheeks. They were hot but she knew she wasn't sick. She was just…what? *Thinking about a smokin' hot cowboy.*

A few minutes later, after a quick check of her supplies on the truck that she might need to deliver a calf, she headed out. With any luck, this wouldn't take long. But then again, it could be another late night.

The cowboy had snuck into her thoughts all day. And the one thing she couldn't figure out was why he'd been out riding before dawn. *Had he been out there all night?*

She told herself it was that curiosity that had him on her mind. Not the fact that every time she thought of him, she felt that surge of attraction that she'd felt the first moment she'd seen him through her sleep-blurred eyes. And she'd felt the tingle of awareness his touch had evoked when he'd taken the cup from her hand.

She slowed as she reached the entrance of the New Horizon Ranch and turned in to the drive. She drove up the long lane toward the huge sandstone home that was on the right and then she turned her truck toward the compound of stables and barns and arenas. This was a showplace and that was more than evident. Maddie, the only partner of the ranch Megan had met, had told her that she and her four partners had been ranch hands who'd inherited the ranch from the owner when he passed away from cancer.

Megan had found the story very touching. He'd obviously trusted them and with good reason, she'd heard good things about the ranch. Their cattle had won major awards at the Houston Livestock Show, the San Antonio shows, and others across the state. The last thing she wanted to do was let something happen to one of their animals. She just hoped whoever had been monitoring the heifer knew what they were looking for and hadn't made the call too late.

She entered one of the barns and could tell by the fresh hay scent and the sweet scent of grain that the place was cleaned often. Sure enough, she saw a man driving a ranch ATV around loaded with hay. He stopped and glanced at her medical bag. "You looking for the birth mother?"

She smiled at his choice of words. "As a matter of fact, I am." The ranch hand nodded toward the arena. "She's in the stalls at the back of the covered arena. First stall. Treb is with her."

"Thanks," she called as he drove away. She headed toward the large covered arena. It was huge, with a sale area for showing and holding auctions. As she headed toward the back where she could see the stalls, she saw a tall cowboy at the opening of the first stall. He turned toward her and her stomach dropped. It was Hot Cowboy.

And he was every bit as good-looking as she'd remembered. It hadn't been her weary mind playing tricks on her.

"So we meet again." She ignored the butterflies in her stomach. What were the odds that he was the one she'd be dealing with?

"Looks that way. I hope you've had a nap." He studied her with serious eyes.

"No nap but loads of coffee. Is she in there?" She nodded past him but she was already on her way.

"She is." He stepped to the side and let her pass in front of him. He briefed her on what had been going on and she agreed that the calf was probably twisted around and in trouble.

The black heifer's coat gleamed. Meagan crossed to the corner where it lay. She felt the cowboy's gaze on her. *Was he judging her? Trying to figure out whether she could do the job?* To her, all livestock was worthy, and all animals, the same as all people, counted. But she also knew in the cattle business that some cattle were more of an investment than others. And her worth as a vet to prize livestock could make or break her reputation.

She ran her hand over the heifer's swollen belly. "Hang on, little mama. This is going to be just fine." Megan reached into her bag for her gloves and then pulled them on.

The cowboy moved to kneel beside her. "I'm here to help." His shoulder brushed hers and she felt that same sizzle of attraction.

"Thanks. She's out of energy but we both know that could change in a moment of pain."

"Yeah, that's not a good place to be. You do your thing down there and I'll keep you from getting flattened."

"Thanks." She didn't waste time talking after that. Instead, she went to work.

Her nerves disappeared as she focused on saving the mother and the baby. She realized quickly into the exam that it was time for action. "You're right. We're going to have to help her deliver this baby with a C-section. This calf is not coming out on its own."

# CHAPTER THREE

Two hours later, Treb stood shoulder to shoulder with Megan as they looked over the now closed stall gate and watched the newborn calf nurse.

"I owe you an apology." He looked down at the amazing woman beside him.

She turned toward him and rested an elbow on a rung of the gate. He was impressed that she was still standing. She'd slept for about three hours in her truck last night and from what she'd told him while they'd worked beside each other delivering the calf, she'd had less than that the night before.

"Really?" she asked. "Why would you say that?"

He resisted the urge to smooth the damp hair from her temple. "That was one tough birth. You kept them both alive. Someone else might have given up and let one or both die."

"So you thought I'd walk away?"

"Hey, I don't know you. I wasn't sure. All I knew was you slept in your truck and you love coffee. I stand corrected. I shouldn't have doubted you."

"I slept in my truck because I'd been up late saving another cow and calf. And I don't just love coffee: I need it to help me make it through my tough schedule." She arched an eyebrow and he felt the challenge in it.

He laughed. "Okay, so you're right—I did know that. But, you seemed a bit…" He grimaced, teasing her.

She narrowed her eyes but a smile wavered playfully on the edges of her lips. "What? Go ahead and finish."

"Flaky."

She laughed. "Wow, you described me as a

*biscuit*."

Her unexpected laugh caught him off guard and the twinkle in her eyes did too. "That isn't a good description. I didn't mean—"

"No. No backtracking. It's fine. I totally see where you'd get that idea. I was a little out of it this morning—still am. Exhaustion will do that." She chuckled again and then turned serious. "But trust me, I know my stuff, tired or rested." She rubbed her forehead with the back of her hand.

"And I know that's true. I made a mistake and that's why I'm apologizing," he said with conviction that he hoped would ease the tension that his other words had helped create. "I didn't give you enough credit. I won't do that again."

"Thank you for saying that. Now, it's getting late and I need to go. I might get a little sleep tonight."

"I hope so. I'm going to make sure the owners here at the ranch know how meticulous you were."

"I appreciate that. I'm working hard to build a good reputation."

"You don't have to worry about that. Have you

met any of the partners?"

"I've met Maddie. She called me out a couple of times to take care of her orphan calves."

"So I'm sure she already knows how fantastic you are. She runs a great program saving those calves."

"Thanks. I'm just doing my job helping the animals."

He followed her out of the building to her truck.

She was being modest and he knew it. She was a miracle worker—that calf had almost no chance to live and she'd saved both mother and calf. She'd impressed the heck out of him.

She had his curiosity up.

"I'll see you later. Call me if you need me."

He watched her leave, just as he'd watched her leave that morning, and there was a heightened sense of readiness inside him…readiness to see her again.

The next morning, Megan pulled her truck to a stop in front of Sam's Diner. She'd gotten another emergency call less than an hour after leaving the New Horizon

Ranch. And so the night had gone: one call after the other. Needless to say, it was a good thing that as of now she was off the clock until Monday morning. She was going to finally get to sleep. But before she drove home, she needed food. Betty would have her hide if she knew Megan hadn't eaten anything since the sandwich the receptionist had brought back to the clinic for her lunch yesterday.

She was starving…and Sam's breakfast was calling her name.

Pushing open the heavy wooden door, she walked into the diner. The scent of frying bacon mixed with the sweet scent of warm cinnamon rolls nearly made her double over with desire. Her stomach growled like a lion. Nobody she'd ever found could make breakfast like Sam Green.

The little jockey-sized man was at the counter and because it was not even six a.m., there wasn't anyone but him and the cook in the back. He turned when she entered and his leathered face lit up in welcome. "Mornin', Doc. You've beat App and Stanley this morning. I think that's a record. And you look like you've had a long one. Again." He scowled as she slid onto a cowhide-covered barstool. "You look whupped," he said as she eyed the coffee he was already pouring into a mug for her.

"I am. And I'll love you for always for this." She took the cup as he placed it in front of her and breathed deeply. "Oh, you are a sweetheart. If you weren't already married, I'd snag you up in a New York minute." She took a cautious sip and savored the heat as it burned its way down her throat.

"See thar, you've just proven how tired you are b'cause that coffee will grow hair on your...*ears* and ain't many women would appreciate that."

She laughed. "I guess you're right. I wouldn't want to grow hair on my ears. But you're wrong—this is wonderful."

"You need some rest," he warned, studying her with concerned eyes.

"I'm on my way to crash as soon as I finish up a breakfast combo."

"You got a deal then. I'll get it ordered."

The door opened. Applegate Thornton and Stanley

Orr hustled in. The two retired oil men ran small ranches in the area but mostly just leased their land out to the larger ranches in the area these days. They could be found most mornings battling it out over a checkerboard at the front window table at Sam's. And today she'd actually beat them. Their expressions of surprise made her laugh.

"Mornin', boys. What took you so long?" she drawled with a smile.

Tall and skinny like a flagpole, App, as everyone called him, set the spittoon on the floor and frowned at her. "Honey." His booming voice almost made her jump. Neither he nor Stanley could hear. "You'll grow old fast if you keep working these kinds of hours. We told Susan the same thing and now she's got a husband and a baby."

"Shor did." Stanley sank into a chair and laid the checkerboard on the table. Shorter and slightly plump, Stanley hitched a bushy brow—his brows had more hair on them than his head had. "You're gonna be old sooner than ya think, girl. You need to have some fun."

Her mother's voice echoed Stanley's and Megan

almost laughed, she was so weary. "The only fun I'm wanting right now is eating some of Sam's good eats and then snuggling into my bed and sleeping till Monday."

Before anyone could say anything else, the door opened again. Of all people to walk inside, it was Treb.

Megan blinked, as if she were dreaming him. Which was understandable considering she hadn't been able to rid herself of thoughts of him all night. The cowboy had helped her with the difficult C-section and she'd been undeniably drawn to him and aware of him next to her the whole time.

"Mornin'," he greeted everyone and strode toward her. His penetrating eyes bore into her.

This morning, he had a dark five o'clock shadow on his jaw and he looked tired. It struck Megan that he carried himself like a military man: straight back, shoulders squared, jaw held high and rigid, and grit in his gaze. He sat down on the stool beside her and laid a hand on the counter.

"So we meet again." He repeated her words of the day before.

"Looks that way. Are you following me?" She was very aware of the way the room now seemed to buzz with electricity. Aware that his hand on the counter was a mere inch from hers as she cuddled the warm coffee mug. All he had to do was lift a finger and he'd be touching her. The thought sent a shiver down her spine. Megan swallowed hard.

"No, but I like the idea."

Megan swallowed the lump that lodged in her throat at his words.

"Coffee, Treb?" Sam pulled her attention away from the man at her side. The diner owner grinned.

"That'd be great." Treb then focused back on her.

"Did you pull another all-nighter?"

She took a drink of coffee. "I did. Did you? You look tired."

"You look like you were up all night," App boomed from the window seat. It would be hard for him and Stanley to hear anything going on at the counter but they were trying.

Treb swiveled his barstool toward her so that he could now focus on everyone in the room from that vantage point. The movement brought him closer to Megan and suddenly she felt as if she'd just run a barrel race without a horse.

"I actually did," he said. "We've got hogs on the ranch and I did a little trapping last night."

"All night?" Stanley asked.

Treb nodded and Megan looked at him in disbelief. "Why?"

"Yeah?" Sam joined in. "All night?"

Treb shrugged. "I'm off today," he said, as if that explained it all. He grinned at her. "I thought if you could do it, I could too. Maybe I'll sleep some today. Are you going to sleep some or did you sleep in your truck again last night?"

"I saved a few animals but had no time to sleep in or out of my truck."

"What was that?" App bellowed, drawing their attention as he spat a sunflower seed into the spittoon. It hit the copper container with an unmistakable zing.

"I spent a couple of hours sleeping in my truck the other night because I got too tired to drive. Treb found me sleeping."

"Like I said," Sam grunted. "You need a backup. What can I get you, Treb?" he asked, shooting her a wrinkled frown of concern.

Megan had learned quickly that Mule Hollow folks didn't mind speaking their minds, especially if something concerned them. It showed they cared. Yes, it sometimes felt nosey but underlying concern softened the intrusion.

"I'll have a full breakfast," Treb said. "You might throw in an extra one of your flaky biscuits." He winked at her.

"Funny," she said, under her breath, as Sam headed to the back with the orders.

"I thought about you all night," he said, for her ears only.

Her stomach dipped and she fought the attraction that arced between them.

"That's not a good idea," she replied in reflex. It wasn't, so why did the knowledge thrill her?

"I agree, but I did it anyway."

"You agree?" She spun toward him and their knees touched.

His lips curved into a devastating smile. "I do. You work all the time—I'm not excited about competing against that."

"Do you doctor buzzards?" App boomed, interrupting Treb's words.

Megan pulled her attention off what Treb had been saying and stared in confusion at App.

"Did you say buzzard?"

"Yup. That's what I asked. Victor's his name. Or at least that's what I've tagged him with. I don't think he can fly. He just mopes around the yard, waitin' on me to throw him some leftovers."

Treb and Megan swiveled their barstools toward App. They bumped legs and Megan laughed softly, feeling unnerved by his nearness. She wanted to blame it on how weary she was…but she wasn't sure that was it. She tried to concentrate on what App was saying and not Treb's nearness.

"Seriously, you have a buzzard?" Treb asked incredulously.

"I didn't go pick him out of a lineup in the pet store but yup, he's been hanging around the barn and

I've been feeding him. He showed up and didn't leave."

Stanley shook his head. "It's disgusting."

"Hey, he looked hurt so I threw some leftovers out and he went at 'em like he was starvin'. Been about a week now, so I named him."

"That is disgusting," Treb agreed.

"Thank ya, Treb," Stanley grumbled. "I told him to get rid of the nasty thing. You should smell it. It stinks to hog heaven."

"And just how do I do that? Shoot him?" App snapped.

"Well, there's a thought," Sam grunted as he came out of the kitchen with Megan and Treb's orders.

"I ain't shootin' Victor." App pinned his gaze on Megan. "Well, do ya?"

She cringed, thinking about the stench of the scavengers that lived off roadkill. "Honestly, I don't know, App. I've never been asked to doctor a buzzard."

"No, you don't. App, what are you thinking?" Treb demanded. "Don't feed it. It'll have to go off and do what it does naturally: eat dead things. And Megan has no business getting up close and personal with it."

"Hey, I have a tough stomach. If I didn't, I couldn't do my job."

"But buzzards are nasty." Treb placed a hand on her arm. "Tell him no."

She didn't like him telling her what to do. She could make up her own mind. But she did like the feel of his hand on her arm.

"App, this conversation is getting a little too out there for a diner," Sam said. "Let the buzzard talk go. Or my business might go to the buzzards."

Megan was glad of the distraction and turned toward her food. The succulent scents rose from the plate—especially the sweet cinnamon goodness of the cinnamon roll. Her stomach growled and as famished as she was, she forgot all talk of buzzards as she picked up the gooey roll. She gazed at it for a split second, just admiring the beauty of it, and then she took a warm, buttery bite.

"Oh my goodness," she mumbled through chews. "This is delicious."

"Thank you. That's my Adela's recipe." Sam's expression softened at the mere mention of his wife. "They're as sweet as she is." His gaze shifted to Treb. "Son, you gonna eat or just stare at Megan while she eats?"

Megan paused chewing and glanced at Treb. If his pink ears were any indication that he'd been caught staring, then he'd been caught. At the moment, he was staring at Sam.

She cleared her throat loudly to draw his attention. "Eat your own, buster," she warned with a wink and then tore off another piece of the sticky bun and stuffed it into her mouth.

A slow grin fanned across his face and his eyes drifted to her lips. Instantly her stomach dipped dangerously once again and she felt breathless. She seemed to never be able to control her reactions around him.

"Yes, ma'am," he drawled. "But there is no way it's going to taste as good as you made that one look."

"Yup, just what I thought," Sam muttered. They both looked at the old cowboy, who grinned. "You two better not be doing that in front of my Adela and her nosey friends unless you're looking for a little meddling to come your way."

"What?" Megan stammered, looking from Sam to Treb. She was suddenly not sleepy or hungry. "We just met. I helped deliver a calf that was really in trouble and that's it."

"That's true," Treb agreed, though she thought she caught a twinkle in his eyes before he looked at Sam.

Sam's grin grew. "I'm simply warning you. 'Cuz sparks will get those three in a dither like nothing you've ever seen."

Megan swallowed her food, though it had suddenly lost its flavor.

"So you saved some calves yesterday?" App slapped a checker down on the board.

Megan was grateful for the distraction from what Sam was saying and would have even welcomed more buzzard talk. "I did," she said over her shoulder. "I almost lost the mama and the baby last night, though. I was so relieved they made it. If they'd not fought hard to survive, they wouldn't have made it. I appreciate the will to fight in humans and animals alike."

"I do too," Treb said.

"Ha," App snapped. "Me too. That's why I'm wonderin' about Victor."

"Give it up, App. He's a buzzard and from what he eats, he should be sick most of the time." Stanley grunted and then jumped a red checker over a black one. "Gotcha, you old coot." He chuckled.

"What!" App studied the board. "You better watch it or I'm gonna get Victor to get all his buddies and come make a visit to your place."

"Ha, yourself!" Stanley laughed. "I ain't rotten enough. You, on the other hand…"

Their bickering faded as Megan's gaze swung to Treb before she could stop it. He looked almost troubled and she wondered what he was thinking—was he worrying about Sam's statement about the posse?

She turned back to finish her food. He did too. They ate in silence and then she took a last sip of her decaf coffee and stood up. "Well, fellas, it's been fun but my bed is calling my name loud and strong."

Treb rose as she stood. "You're going to be alright

going home? You look really tired."

"I'm fine. The food and the company helped. I can make it to the place I'm renting. It's just on the outskirts of town." She told him the country road the little house and acre were located on.

"I know that place. Our ranch has land just past there."

"Really? Well, it's a lovely little place and I can have my animals."

"I've seen a golden retriever on the front porch."

"That's Archie. He's watching over the place."

"So that's Archie."

"Yes. He's a sweetheart and probably worrying about me right now." She pulled some money out of her pocket and laid it on the counter. "Bye, y'all."

"You take care, Doc," Sam called.

"Thanks, Sam. It was great!"

Treb laid money on the bar and to her surprise said his good-byes too. He followed her out the door. "You don't have to follow me. Sam's got the wrong idea now. I—"

"Would you like to go out to dinner sometime?"

She halted on the boardwalk. Butterflies erupted in her chest like geese off a pond. "Are you asking me on a date?"

His lips hitched into a devastating smile. "I am. But that may not be anything you're interested in where I'm concerned."

She yawned. "Sorry." She laughed.

"That bad, huh?" He chuckled and her insides warmed.

"It's probably not a good idea."

"From where I'm standing, it's a very good idea."

"But—I'm so busy. Just like you pointed out earlier. There's no time."

"How about tonight? Since you're getting rest today and you're not on call. I'm off too."

She should say no. She should.

She really should.

But…she couldn't help herself. "I warn you it's just a date. I don't do more than that." *What was she doing?*

His lips quirked up at the edge. "All I'm asking is for a date. I'd like to get to know you better."

Her heart was doing the rumba in her chest and her mouth went dry. "Okay then. Tonight it is. Now I must sleep." *You mean run.*

He grinned. "I'll pick you up at six. How's that?"

"I'll be waiting." *This is nuts.*

Maybe but it was too late now to back out.

# CHAPTER FOUR

Treb was still smiling when he stopped by the ranch before he headed to the bunkhouse. He wanted to tell Rafe and Dalton about the hogs.

It was just past six, the time that all the partners and ranch hands all gathered up and then headed to the various jobs that were lined out for the day.

Maddie pulled in behind him and jumped from her truck. She was a ranch partner and had her calf program on the ranch but she and her husband Cliff lived across town on their ranch. He helped Cliff out every once in a while with the professional rodeo bulls that he raised.

"Hey, Treb," she greeted him as she strode his way. She gathered up her long, dark hair into a ponytail as she spoke. Her sun-bronzed arms were lean and toned from the hard work that she did with the cattle. They reminded him of Megan's arms. She was a hard worker, too, and wrestling with livestock and equine like she did was no lightweight's career.

"Hey yourself, boss lady." He grinned at her. "You look happy this morning."

She placed her hands on her hips. "It's a gorgeous day and I just had a good morning kiss from my man, so of course I look happy." She seemed to sparkle as she talked about Cliff. She was a great gal and Cliff was one lucky man to be loved by a woman like her.

He wanted that kind of love. "Cliff's a lucky man is all I can say."

"Thank you, buddy. I'm the blessed one. You're going to make some gal lucky one day too. Soon I hope."

They entered the barn. Dalton came out of a stall, leading his horse. "Lucky gal? Who's a lucky gal?"

"I am," Maddie crooned. "But I'm telling Treb he's going to make a gal lucky one day. It's time for you to start dating."

"I've told him that too," Dalton agreed.

Treb had not meant to get this conversation going but everyone would know soon enough. Talk traveled fast in a tiny town. If anyone so much as saw them together, it would travel like a grass fire. "As a matter of fact, I've got a date tonight."

"Whoo-hoo!" Maddie hooted. "Who?"

"Who?" Rafe and then Ty appeared from other stalls. It suddenly sounded as if the stable were full of owls as they all echoed Maddie.

"Megan, the new vet in town."

Rafe grinned. "It's about time. That's all I can say."

"Agreed," Ty said.

"Oh, I like her," Maddie gushed. "I bet y'all get on good."

"Maybe so. And as much as I'd like to stand here and talk to y'all about my love life, I'm tired and going home to catch some shut-eye. I'm just coming in from tracking hogs all night. I wanted to let y'all know that you're going to need traps and I can do all that starting tomorrow if you want. They're shredding that area and something needs to be done soon."

"That sounds good," Dalton said, and Rafe and the others agreed.

They talked about it a bit more and then he headed out. Dalton walked him back to his truck.

"Man, I'm really glad you're starting to date."

"Don't be so shocked." Treb hadn't expected his love life to be such a big topic of excitement for everyone.

"You haven't dated since you got here. What I'm really thinking is that it's about time. You work too much, so this is a good thing."

"I've just been settling in." It was true. "I don't plan to be single all my life. I need to give my mom some grandchildren since it's just me now." He felt the loss of his brother in so many ways.

"I hear you. I haven't had a biological grandchild for mine yet, but marrying Rae Anne and getting her two children in the deal has been a great blessing for me and my mom. Even has my parents thinking about moving this direction because they don't see the kids enough." Dalton chuckled.

"I can see my mom doing that. After she lost my brother in Afghanistan, she's had a rough go of it. I feel the pressure to give her the grandchildren she craves. Especially after I added to her stress by joining up right after we got the word that Mark had died."

"So that's what happened. Man, I'm sorry."

"Thanks." Treb shrugged; he hadn't talked much about his past. "Mark was the best. It's been hard." He'd thought about Mark a lot today. Ever since Megan had said she appreciated the will to fight in animals and people. That had been Mark. So blamed intent on protecting everyone.

In many ways, Treb felt as though he was playing catch-up to his big brother now. But that was okay. He'd respected his brother more than anyone he'd ever known. He got into his truck. "I'm glad everything worked out for you and Rae Anne." He needed to change the subject. He wasn't to the point where he could go too deep into his personal business.

"Yeah, me too. It was rough there for a while but everything worked out."

Treb wanted that. Wanted what the partners had all found.

And a date with the beautiful veterinarian was exactly where he needed to start.

Archie's barking woke Megan from a dead sleep.

She registered that there had been a knock but she didn't react immediately. As deep in sleep as she'd been, it took a moment to pull out of it. When the knock came again, she sat up and everything came into focus as she glanced at the clock.

Six o'clock.

*"Six o'clock!* Holy smokes," she muttered, and practically fell out of bed. She caught a glance at her disheveled appearance in the mirror. Tried to push her wild hair down a bit and then headed for the door. *So much for the date.* He'd take one look at her now and run for the hills.

Treb was about to knock again when she yanked

the door open. He stepped back when he saw her and she laughed at his reaction.

"Sorry. I just literally rolled out of bed."

"Are you okay?"

She felt her cheeks burn. "I'm fine. I crashed. Your knock woke me up."

"I'm sorry about that. You obviously needed to sleep. Maybe we should do this another time."

"No!" she said too quickly. "I mean, it won't take me long to jump in the shower and I'm famished. When I come out of hibernation after a long time, I'm starving. Seems like I'm starving every time you see me."

"Then you go get ready and I'll make sure you're fed soon."

"Great. And I see you've met Archie."

"We are great friends at this point. I thought he wasn't going to let me get out of my truck. But I talked him into it."

"Really? That's unusual." She watched Treb lean down and rub Archie on the head. He lapped up the loving Treb gave him.

Treb grinned at her. "What can I say? I have a way with animals."

"Obviously. I mean, Archie isn't the best guard dog but he is protective and doesn't usually befriend someone until he sees *me* befriend them."

Treb's smile grew wider. "He just sensed you had a thing for me."

She laughed. "It seems the man has a sense of humor."

"Hey, I was speaking the truth. You know I'm winning you over."

She very nearly got lost in that smile. "Um, I think I better go get dressed if we're going to go eat. Come in and make yourself at home."

He followed her inside. "Take your time. You have a nice place. Homey."

She glanced around, trying to see it through a stranger's eyes. "Thanks. I try. I have cousins down in the Round Top area who live and breathe their junk business. They always call me when they have something they think I'll love."

"Junk business? I don't see junk here."

She laughed. "We endearingly call it junk but it's taking old stuff and repurposing it for use now. Trash to treasure, antiques with a twist. Things like that. If you've ever heard of *Junk Gypsies,* well, they're kind of similar. Their place is called Junk Sister Paradise." She was rambling. Why was she rambling?

Because Treb's very presence had sucked all the air out of the room and she felt...jittery and excited about the evening.

She kept her teeth locked down on her lip so she wouldn't ramble again. That slow smile she liked spread across his face.

"Are you nervous?" His voice was slightly husky, which led her to think he wasn't immune to the things she was feeling.

"Maybe a little. I haven't gone on a date in a very long time."

His expression slackened. "That's unbelievable. Me either. That had to be by choice on your part."

The man had a deep-toned voice that resonated inside her. "In many ways, yes, it was by my choice." It was simpler to say that. She was surprised that he hadn't dated in a while either.

"I bet you've had plenty of offers. So why'd you decide to have dinner with me?"

"I guess it's weird to say I liked the way we got off on the wrong foot but yet, you didn't give up. And we're just going out—no heavy stuff. Why did you ask me?"

"Other than the obvious, let's just say we respect the same things. I like the way you handle yourself. And you believe all life matters. I like that. We need more of that in this world right now."

His eyes shadowed and she wondered what had crossed his mind in that moment. Because the man was hitting all the right notes and it was music to her ears. More than he would ever know. "I like you, Treb. You strike me as one of the good guys."

The shadow was there again. "Thank you. I try to be. I have a brother who died and he was one of them... I try to continue the trend but his shoes are very big and hard to fill."

*So that was it.* "I'm sorry about your brother. What happened to him?"

"He was in the army. Special ops too. A mission went wrong and he took the hit... I didn't mean to get into all of this. You go get ready and let's find a nice place to eat. That's why I'm here."

"I thought you might have been in the military. Your brother was a brave man."

"Yes, he was."

"Thank you for serving. I'm glad you made it home."

He nodded and that shadow crossed his eyes again. "Me too."

Not knowing what else to say, she hurried to her room. She took a fast shower and then tried on five different tops to go with her dress jeans that she opted for rather than slacks. She finally settled on a soft lavender sleeveless top that hung mid-thigh and then she pulled on her favorite pair of sandals. Tonight wasn't a boot night. Her toes longed for freedom because they'd been trapped inside boots twenty-four seven for the last few weeks.

A close inspection revealed the major need for a quick coat of fresh paint. She sank to the edge of her bed and hurriedly did a touch-up coat. Not the best but it would have to do. She was a simple kind of gal and with her line of work, she wasn't one to always get to enjoy all the girly things like manicures and pedicures. Besides, it wasn't as if the man was going to get that close to her toes.

She applied a touch of makeup, fluffed her hair with a blow dryer and then stared at herself in the mirror. "Why are you so nervous?" she demanded. But she knew what it was…something about this guy felt different and she wasn't sure what that meant.

But it was a little scary to her and she wasn't sure why.


Treb walked around Megan's kitchen and living room, trying to get more of a sense of what made Megan tick. A basket of rocks sat on the kitchen counter—further inspection revealed that they looked washed and shined. Nothing about them was special as far as he could see but there they sat in a basket. He would have to ask about that. A few photos were on the counter of

Megan and a woman who looked like an older sister.

He studied her oddly shaped coffee table and realized it was made from an old baby grand piano and he smiled while he looked at it. He realized that was one of the things that drew him to Megan...she was unexpected. From that first moment he'd found her sleeping in her truck, she'd kept him on his toes and his curiosity up.

He'd dated very little since coming back from Afghanistan but lately the loneliness that he felt in having no one to share his life with had weighed on him. It was more than just giving his mom grandchildren.

He was ready to find a wife for himself; he just hadn't felt inspired until Megan.

She was totally not what he was looking for. She worked long hours, loved her career. She'd clearly stated that she wasn't interested in marriage and marriage was all he was interested in.

So what was he doing going out with her?

He had no idea. He just couldn't help himself.

The bedroom door opened and he turned.

Immediately, all the air in his lungs froze. She was stunning, with her caramel colored hair hanging down in waves about her shoulders. She was a vision. He yanked his hat off. "You are one beautiful woman."

She smiled, almost shyly. "Thank you. Are you ready?"

"Oh yeah."

That made her laugh.

"Me too."

They gave Archie a head rub, locked the door and left the golden retriever curled up and watchful on the front porch.

Within moments, they were on their way. Treb's heart hadn't slowed down its rampage and he glanced at Megan after a few moments.

She smiled. "What? Is my hair messed up or something?"

"Darlin', there is not one thing messed up about you." And he meant every word of it.

He'd just recently gotten back his faith. It had taken him a long time to get over the anger that had consumed him when Mark was killed. But God had waited patiently for him to get over his anger. And now, Treb wanted nothing more than to thank Him for putting this beautiful, vibrant woman into his life. That smile and sparkling eyes holding his attention had him feeling blessed. He watched the road.

"You're laying it on a little thicker than I was expecting," she said.

He glanced at her. "I'm only telling the truth. And I don't lie."

"I don't either."

"That's what I thought. So, I figured we'd ride over to Ranger and have something to eat there."

"I'm easy. I'm just looking for a nice evening, a good meal, and good company and I'll be one happy girl."

"Two out of three I can promise you. But the company is something you'll have to judge from your viewpoint. But I'll try real hard."

"Fair enough, cowboy. I'll let you know what I think in a little while." She winked.

He smiled as he drove. *This was going to be a good night.*

# CHAPTER FIVE

Megan had gained control of her jitters by the time they reached the restaurant. It was a nice place overlooking a lake and they were led to a table on the deck. Lights were strung overhead and a guy sung sixties rock-n-roll on the other side of the deck. It was exactly the kind of place to help her relax and energize at the same time.

"This is perfect," she told Treb as he held out her chair for her. Always the gentleman, she was learning.

"I thought you might like it. Maddie actually told me about it. This is my first time here too. But she assured me it was exactly what I was looking for."

"I'll have to thank her. There are five partners, right? I've just met Maddie."

"Five is right. It's a big ranch and they do a great job running it."

"It takes a lot of you to do the work, it looks like."

"True. There's several other hands who work there and we stay busy."

The waitress came and they ordered their food. When she left, Treb leaned back in his chair and studied her. "So you know about my brother and my mother. What about your family?"

Megan toyed with the napkin in her lap. "I have two sisters and my mother. I've never known who my dad was. He and my mother split up when my sisters and I were very small and he never came around. I don't remember much about him since I'm the youngest."

"Sorry about that. It must have been hard growing up without your dad."

"You could say that." Her sarcastic side came out on that one. "In more ways than you can imagine. My mother married three times during my stint at home and the drama of it all was over the top. My sisters have followed the pattern and both have gone through divorces. My middle sis remarried but is in a battle right now and will probably be divorced again by next year from all that I gather. The drama is out of this world. I try to stay clear of it all."

Why was she opening up to him like this? Was she trying to emphasize that this was a date only and she was not the marrying kind? If so, then she was doing a bang-up job of it.

"As far as I'm concerned, being single is the way to go," she added, just in case he hadn't gotten the picture.

He didn't say anything for a moment, just took it all in as he studied her in the romantic light of the deck. In the background, *Smoke Gets In My Eyes* was being sung and it only added to the romantic feel of the night that she'd pretty much just destroyed with her loud mouth.

"I feel your pain," he said after a moment. He reached across the table and laid his hand over hers and gave it a quick squeeze. There was absolutely no judgment in his words or actions.

She didn't normally talk to anyone about her personal life, so she was a little baffled that she had opened up to him so much.

Nerves maybe?

*Caution, caution.*

She clearly heard her common sense chanting in the back of her thoughts but she'd enjoyed herself more than she had in a very long time. Treb was the real deal; he was a great guy. By the time the waitress asked whether they'd like dessert, she had calmed her nerves again and just enjoyed his company.

They both declined dessert, though she found herself wanting to order the Italian Cream Cake just so they could spend more time together. *This was crazy.*

They were leaving the restaurant and Treb placed his hand on her lower back again. The gentle pressure there made her so very aware of him; she wanted to turn and feel his arms around her completely.

*Caution.*

He opened the truck door for her and held her

elbow as she scooted into the high seat, just as he'd done earlier. This time he didn't move away immediately.

"I really enjoyed tonight." His voice turned husky.

She could feel her pulse pound. "Me too."

His gaze dropped to her lips and her mouth went dry with the tempting thought of kissing him. She was single, young, and in control of her life. She could kiss a man if she felt like it.

Only, something very, very strong told her kissing Treb could alter all of her control.

And that would be setting herself up for possible drama of her own that she'd witnessed her family deal with over and over.

Her pulse raged harder as the moments and thoughts flew. Then he moved away, closing the door before he strode around the front of the truck to slip behind the steering wheel.

Disappointment and relief tangled together inside her as he cranked the truck.

Before he pulled out of the driveway, he cocked his head to look at her. "This may be too early to say this but you shake me up, Megan."

She laughed at his candor and the knowledge that she wasn't the only one confused by the pull between them.

"I can say likewise," she murmured.

After that, they were both quiet as he drove back to her house. The tension inside the truck was as thick as Houston humidity.

Megan hadn't expected this and she sure didn't know what to do about it.

All the way home, one thought stood out above all the others…she wanted Treb to take her in his arms and kiss her breathless.

She reminded herself again that she was single and this was a healthy female reaction to a man she was so very much attracted to. It wasn't as if she'd completely sworn off the opposite sex. She just wasn't thinking long-term or intimate relationships. She had self-discipline by the truckloads and yet, her eyes kept straying across the truck to him…

"So, you're back on duty tomorrow. Working all kinds of hours," he asked as he pulled into her drive. "I go back on call on Sunday night but have Sunday to myself."

He parked the truck and turned toward her, making no move to get out. He laid his arm on the seat; his hand rested next to her shoulder. "So are you holding up okay?" He picked up a strand of her hair and rubbed it between his fingertips.

Megan's attention was riveted to those fingers gently rubbing her hair. She swallowed hard and tried to focus on his question. "I'm holding up fine. I'm a big girl." She was not holding up to him, though.

A slow smile slid across his face. "I really like your attitude."

She liked his eyes, his voice, that smile…his attitude too.

She reached for the door handle. She needed to move or there was a strong likelihood that she was about to throw herself into his arms and kiss the daylights out of him.

"I think it's time I headed inside," she said. "It's an early day tomorrow." She pushed the door open. The night air cooled her heated skin as she hopped from the truck.

Treb was coming around the front of the truck. *Oh, this was not good. A girl could only have so much self-control!*

Archie came out of the shadows and went straight to him. She took advantage of that and got to her back door while he petted the dog. She had the key in the lock by the time he moved up behind her.

The heat of his nearness had her skin break out in goose bumps. Anticipating that he might kiss her, she turned and found herself very nearly in his arms, just as she'd been envisioning all evening.

"I had a great time tonight."

"I did too." She swallowed hard. He wasted no time drawing her into his arms and she went willingly—despite common sense yelling *traitor* in the background.

He smelled of spicy aftershave that enticed her to snuggle closer.

"I hope you don't mind," he murmured and then lowered his lips to hers.

Instantly, she melted against him. Surrendered to

the feel of his strength and the desire in his kiss. It had been far too long since she'd felt anything like this. Treb's kiss was firm, commanding as he angled his mouth over hers and shattered every barrier she had against why this wasn't a good idea.

Instead of drawing away, her arms went around his neck and drew him closer to her. His heart pounded against hers and her knees went weak.

Her world was spinning when he broke away, looking as stunned as she felt. They stared at each other in silence. She fought her own war of control like none she'd ever fought before.

Treb stepped back from her, but held her firmly by the shoulders. His eyes in the lamplight remained dazed—as dazed as she knew her own had to be.

"Do you kiss all the girls like that?" She finally managed the breathless question.

He shook his head slowly as a tempting smile played at the edges of his lips. "There's never been a kiss like that."

They stared at each other. He started to pull her close again and stopped, his brows knitting endearingly.

"I better not do that again. Not right now. If I start again, I might not be able to stop."

She understood the feeling. She'd lost all good sense during that kiss. "Agreed. I better go inside."

His warm hands rubbed her shoulders, kneading them, melting her all the more.

Then he let her go and stepped back. As if the extra foot between them could break the connection.

It didn't.

"Thanks for the night," she offered lamely. What was she supposed to say? *Thanks for the kiss of a lifetime. The kiss to end all kisses...the life-changing kiss...*

He reached around her, twisted the door handle and then pushed her door open. "Good night, Megan. I had a great night."

His intoxicating scent wrapped around her. She gave him a wilted smile, one tied up in emotions she completely did not understand. Had no experience with. And then she stepped into her kitchen, called Archie in, and shut the door.

For the first time in her life, she didn't trust herself.

*She wanted Treb Carson.*

Wanted everything there was about him and she barely knew him. It was unbelievable and she did not understand it at all.

She touched her lips with her fingertips. They still tingled with the feel of Treb's lips on hers. How could one kiss turn her world, her plans—*everything*—upside down?

# CHAPTER SIX

Treb squinted in the brilliant sunlight two days after he'd kissed Megan. Since that kiss, everything he thought of seemed to fall into two categories: before the kiss and after the kiss.

He'd been smiling ever since and as he drove the truck, hauling a load of feed out to where he'd set up hog traps, he was still grinning like a fool. But he didn't feel like a fool—he felt as if he was the luckiest man alive.

Keith Urban was crooning a love song on the radio and was just one more reason he had Megan on his mind. Memories of their date and the great time they'd had played in between the moments that the kiss replayed in his thoughts. They'd had so much in common and he'd enjoyed talking to her. She was opinionated, passionate about her work, and caring. She intrigued him and he liked everything about her.

Especially the way she kissed…

He whistled as he pulled the truck up to the hog feeder. Moving from the inside of the truck, he climbed into the truck bed and reached over to the top of the feeder and opened the hatch. He picked up the first fifty-pound bag of feed, opened it and then poured the corn into the feeder. When he finished, he closed the lid and checked the feed cycle. All the while, he was distracted by thoughts of Megan.

He had it bad.

He told himself he shouldn't have kissed her. But it was impossible not to want to and he'd had a moment of weakness. She'd come enthusiastically into his arms—which was irresistible. And when she'd wrapped her arms around his neck and kissed him back—that was it. Dear heaven above, he'd thought he'd died and gone there.

He'd melted inside with the pure sweetness and passion of her response.

That was what he was coming to know about Megan. She was a work in contradictions: reserved yet passionate, soft but strong, and so much more.

There was just something undeniable about the way she affected him. He couldn't stop thinking about her. He'd gone to bed with her on his mind, and needless to say hadn't slept well. But for the first time in a very long time, he'd had something other than war, loss, and regret keeping him awake.

Sometime late into the night when he'd finally drifted into sleep, he'd had a smile on his lips. And it had reappeared the instant his eyes had opened to the new day because his thoughts went instantly to her. It had been the same last night.

He ignored the weak alarm in the back of his thoughts telling him that she was completely not the right woman for him. He was looking for a woman with home and family on her mind. One who wanted and was ready to have children and settle down.

Megan was a workaholic—who loved her work. She didn't have plans for anything he wanted.

She'd point-blank stated that she wasn't looking for marriage.

Her not being right for him couldn't get any plainer than that.

He had a life to get on with…and being suddenly obsessed with a workaholic vet put a big kink in his plans.

The problem was he didn't care. He wanted to feel her in his arms again. He wanted to taste her lips again and he wanted to see whether the kiss had been as amazing as he remembered.

The ding of his phone had him glancing at the screen. He picked it up immediately. "Hey, Maddie."

"Glad I caught you, Treb. Look, I have a chance at a date night with my guy tonight and then a horse show in Stevensville for the next few days. We're going to mix a little business and pleasure. Could you work a little overtime and take care of my babies for me while we're away? You're one of the only ones I trust with them."

"I can sure do that. Would be my pleasure to take care of all your little babies."

She raised and nurtured the orphaned baby calves on the ranch and from the auctions. Her program was a true endeavor of her heart. And he knew from what Megan had said that she liked it too.

"You're amazing and I knew I could count on you. How'd your date go? Yes, it is true—I do not deny it: I am a nosey girl."

He laughed at that. "It went very well."

"Awesome. Love is in the air around here so you need to jump in because it's wonderful. Are you taking her to the Cattleman's Ball?"

"Maddie, I can take it from here."

"Okay, okay, if you say so. I just thought you might be rusty and need some suggestions."

"I'm fine."

"I better warn you that Norma Sue and Esther Mae were down at the diner today at lunch with Adela and they were talking about the two of you. So be warned. Talk to you later and thanks again. I owe you."

Maddie was in love and wanted everyone to have

what she had, so doing a little matchmaking seemed to come naturally to her. But now matchmakers in town were talking about him and Megan. He knew that not long after he'd moved here they were looking for the right girl for him. He hadn't exactly known what to think about that then. He'd since learned that they were pretty busy with their matchmaking hobby and he hadn't worried too much about it. And it still didn't worry him.

He had stayed away from Megan for two days. He'd forced himself to give them space but he hadn't liked it. He wanted to see her and as he ended the call with Maddie, he knew it was hopeless. It was time to see Megan.

Instead of putting his phone into his pocket, he dialed her number. His spirits lifted higher just dialing her number. It was time to see her again.

Past time.

Megan stared at the stallion that glared at her from the center of the round pen. "You think you're a big tough guy, don't you? Well, you might be, but I'm here to help you. If you'll let me."

She'd been behind all morning and this fella had been loaded into the pen an hour earlier with a major bite on his hip. He'd gotten it when he and another stallion had gotten together and decided to see who was the head honcho of the mares. She wasn't sure whether he'd won or not...she hadn't seen the other guy but it had to look better than this fella.

She took a step forward. "Come on, buddy. You might have been on the losing end of the fight and are probably feeling out of sorts from that. But don't take it out on me. I'm here to help."

He pawed a front hoof and snorted. Megan halted at his warning.

Betty had left to pick up lunch and for once the clinic was quiet. The calving was almost over and it seemed that the small animal practice might be calming down also. Megan was so ready for a normal schedule. If she got this horse treated, then she wouldn't be behind on her afternoon and might just get off on time.

Her common sense told her to wait until there was at least someone else around. It was the smart thing to do just in case something went wrong. But, the slight possibility that she'd actually get off at a normal hour today won out.

"I'm going to tend your wound now, buddy. You'll be happy when I'm done. I promise." She'd done this alone plenty of times. If she had to, she could sedate him but she really hated to do that. If he moved three steps over and entered the narrow alley opening, he would move into the head stall, where she could immobilize him while she doctored him.

Determined, she waved her arms and moved toward him. His nostrils flared, ears flattened, and with each step she took, he grew more agitated. He pawed the earth.

Megan halted. "Okay, so you know I'm the vet. Not the trainer. I just need you to take a couple of steps to the left," she said soothingly. "I know your hip has to hurt despite the fact that you're putting on the tough guy act for me."

She took another step toward him and the stubborn

horse charged her.

"Hah!" Megan yelled, trying to turn him back, waving her arms like a loon flapping in the wind. He paused and then spun away from her, but then he kicked out like a rodeo bronc bucking off a rider. She dove out of the way but a hoof caught her... Pain exploded in her hand as she felt bones crack.

She stumbled back and fell hard to the ground, jarring every inch of her body. The horse spun back toward her and for the first time in a very long time, fear raced through her.

Treb pulled into the vacant parking lot of the veterinarian clinic and had to wonder whether they'd closed up for the day. Odd, but he was just used to seeing at least one truck in the lot during this time of day. Deciding to bypass the parking lot, he drove around back where large animals were unloaded. He had called Megan twice and gotten her voicemail, which was strange considering she wore it in a holster at her hip.

He'd decided to drive on into town and ask her in person whether she wanted to go to the dance with him. It gave him an excuse to see her today. He'd known he was taking a chance on her being out in the field but it was lunch time, so he hoped she was in the office. He spied her truck parked next to the pens and parked beside it. Anticipation buzzed through him as he opened his door and jumped to the ground. He rounded the end of his truck at a fast clip. He spotted Megan on the ground in the pen. His blood chilled seeing the freaked-out stallion charging toward her.

As if in slow motion, he watched Megan clutch a hand to her chest protectively as she struggled to one knee. He could tell she was hoping to make a run for the protection of the fence but clearly she wasn't going to make it.

Treb bolted for the iron rungs of the pen, yelling orders at the black stallion. He tried to draw its attention to him even as he knew he was too late. He clamored over the fence and threw himself over the top rail and into the pen. Megan threw herself to the dirt and rolled toward him and away from the horse's hooves as they crashed down where she'd been. The horse kept coming, though, and caught her leg. Treb's yell finally caught the animal's attention and it spun and raced to the far side of the pen. Treb reached Megan in that moment and dropped to his knees beside her. She lay with her face to the ground and her arms covered her head.

Treb's heart pounded out of his chest as he looked down at her still form. Gently, he took her shoulders. "Megan, I'm here, honey. How bad are you hurt?"

She groaned and then flopped to her back and stared up at him. She was breathing hard and pain clearly registered on her face. "I cannot believe how stupid I was."

That took him by surprise. "I think rolling was pretty smart." He reached for her leg where he knew the hooves had struck her and saw her jeans were ripped.

She flinched.

"How bad do you think? Can you walk?"

She held the wrist of her left hand.

"Is your arm hurt too?"

"My hand could possibly be broken. My leg…I think is just going to be really sore for a few days."

He had no idea why she'd been alone in the pen with the high-strung horse and he didn't like it at all. But now was not the time to bring that up. "Come on. Let's get you to the hospital."

He took her right arm and wrapped another arm around her waist, and then eased her to a standing position, continuing to hold her as she tested her leg.

A hiss of pain escaped her lips. "I don't think it's broken but it's roughed up pretty bad."

He gave her a gentle hug. "It'll be okay. Let's go."

She glanced at the horse and then back up at him. "I need you to help me over to the head stall. I have everything set up there. If you can move him into it, I can fix his wound before we go."

"Seriously? You're barely standing up and your hand is probably broken but you want to doctor the horse that did this to you? I don't think so. We're going to the hospital."

"No. I can put all my weight on my good leg and I'm right-handed. With your help, I can help that horse. He's hurting. That's why he's behaving like this."

He stared at her. "And what if I get hurt?"

She gave a small smile. "You won't and you know it."

They locked gazes for a long moment. "Stubborn woman," he said in an exasperated breath. And grudgingly acknowledged that he admired her for taking this stand.

"Please."

"Fine. Come on." He eased her across the arena to where she had her supplies laid out on a tray.

She took hold of the rail. "Okay, I'm fine. Go run him in here."

He could not help himself; he leaned in and brushed his lips across hers. Her sharp intake of breath told him he'd startled her—but so be it, because he'd needed that kiss.

He'd thought in the moments it had taken him to

get to her that he might have lost her. And he'd only just found her.

From the moment of thinking he'd lost her to the moment of seeing what kind of heart she truly had, he knew he wasn't going to let go of her without a fight.

And that fight started now.

# CHAPTER SEVEN

Megan's lips tingled from his gentle kiss as she watched Treb stride back out into the arena and move toward the horse. She hurt all over and yet he'd just sent a sweet, sweet sensation soaring through her.

Cowboy that he was, he held his arms open wide, making himself appear bigger and impenetrable to the horse as he strode steadily toward it. The stinker took one look at the big bad cowboy and bolted straight toward the corner, where it was herded easily into the opening of the chute and walked straight into the stall.

The moment it stuck its head out the far end of the stall, she used her good hand to pull the lever. It gently squeezed in the sides of the chute until it held the stallion still.

The horse turned its wide, pained and frightened eyes her way and Megan hurt for it.

"Calm down, now. This won't take long and yes, I know you didn't mean to hurt me. I'm going to fix you up and you'll be all better and back to your sweet self again…you are sweet, aren't you? If you're not, then you should really think about it because being ornery isn't going to make you any friends."

Treb's husky chuckle had her glancing over to find him very near her.

"I'm here if you need me, Doc."

His words filled her and she turned back to focus on the job in front of her. As she worked, she hyper aware of him and in a strange way, that helped her not feel the pain radiating from her injured hand. She'd rested it on the railing as she worked to keep it elevated because that helped the throbbing a little. She was so not focused on that, though; with the horse and Treb, there was plenty to keep her mind off her own pain.

And thinking of Treb…well, she couldn't shake the feeling that they were a great team. A team that she could truly and honestly get used to.

That was territory that she'd never treaded down before. Territory that she wasn't sure she would ever go down. Her past was so littered with unsuccessful friends and family who hadn't made it, not to mention her mom and sisters. It had always just seemed simpler and easier to focus on herself and her wants and not include a second party.

But as she finished up on the horse and Treb released it back into the pen, her thoughts entertained that there could be a possibility of at least opening up to Treb.

When she had finished, he looked down at her and warned, "I'm going to try picking you up. If it hurts your leg in any way, let me know."

"You don't have to do that—" she protested, but

he had her in his arms before she finished talking. And once there—she was content to stay.

Treb carried Megan toward his truck. By the expression on her face, he could tell that she was in pain but she was a trouper and didn't complain.

"How are you doing?"

"I'm fine."

He didn't bother arguing but continued the short distance to the truck. Pulling open the passenger door with the hand of the arm he had beneath her knees, he slipped her into the seat as carefully as he could and buckled her in. Then he hurried to his side of the truck and climbed in and headed out. He drove carefully over the rough rock of the parking lot, trying not to bounce her around too much. Once he was on the hard pavement, he hit the gas and picked up speed. It was time to get her to the hospital.

The only problem with Mule Hollow being such a small town was it had no medical care. The closest hospital was in Ranger, an hour away. This made emergencies hard. One day the town needed to at least have a nurse or a physician's assistant. It might be time to petition the town to consider seeking out some kind of medical care. He planned to initiate the conversation.

"Thank you for rescuing me."

He glanced at her. Irritation pricked at the edge of his thoughts. He spoke carefully. "I'm glad I showed up when I did. Why were you attempting to work on that horse with no one else around?'

"I'm the vet. It needed attention."

"Why did the owner drop it off and not help?"

Her brows knitted together. "Because I'm the vet. And they had work to do. And that's my job, remember?"

"But you could have been killed, Megan. That horse was in pain and felt threatened and it had nowhere to run. That made it a triple threat." He glanced from the road back to her.

She glared at him. "Do you not think I know the behaviors of a horse?"

There was pain in her voice and he hated that he'd just had to let his frustrations out at her. But this was her life they were talking about.

"I know you do and that's why I'm asking you— what were you thinking?"

"I was thinking that I was helping the horse. That he needed help. And why are you questioning me? I don't need your approval. I was simply thanking you for saving me."

Treb's temper spiked and he gripped the steering wheel tighter. She was telling him to back off and he couldn't do it because he couldn't deny it any longer— he cared for her. "You should have asked for help. Don't you get it? You could have been killed," he repeated. "That horse was out of his mind." He focused forward before he said too much. "Let's just get you to the hospital and get your hand fixed up. We can talk about this later." He shot a glance at Megan.

She had her face turned away from him, staring out at the passing scenery. "There's no need to talk about it later. I'm not looking for your approval or disapproval. When we get to the hospital, you can drop me off at the door and head back to your responsibilities. I'm not one of those."

That did it. "Why are you so stubborn?"

"That also is not your business."

"No way—*no way* am I going to drop you off at the emergency room. If you think I'd just leave you, then you have a lot to learn about me."

"I want you to."

"Well, honey, I've got news for you—you're stuck with me. And you're right. Maybe because I'm upset and worried about you, I'm getting a little overbearing but it's just because I care."

*There, he said it.* He turned in to the parking lot of the hospital and drove to the entrance. "Hold on. I'll be right back." He barreled out of the truck and jogged around to her side, where she'd already pushed open the door.

Her face was pale as he took her into his arms. *Dear Lord, he could hold her for the rest of his life.* When she looked up at him, his heart melted.

"Let's get you fixed up," he said tersely and strode into the hospital to get his woman some help.

Four hours later, Megan limped out of the ER with Treb's gentle hand cupping her elbow, giving her his support. It had been a tense time for a little while there but she'd found herself feeling horrible for snapping at him. He'd been nothing but helpful and yes, he'd gotten more personal than she'd wanted him to but why did his questions needle her so much? Was it because she'd been asking herself the same questions?

She didn't like being called on her mistake. She was so independent...translated, that'd be stubborn. She hadn't let anyone get close enough to her in her adult life to care enough to hold her accountable for her actions. And here Treb had barged through the wall she'd surrounded herself with and shown that he cared.

That terrified her far worse than the angry stallion had.

They didn't talk much on the way home. She was lost in her own thoughts and he seemed to be too.

Once they arrived back at the clinic, he followed her to the rear entrance.

"Megan, are you okay?"

His soft question halted her at the door. "I'm fine. Once you gave me an apology and I'm thinking this time I owe you one for the way I acted on the way to the hospital."

"No apology needed. You had a nosey guy butting into your life and we were both stressed out. I'm just really concerned for you."

"And that's the problem. I'm not used to having someone worry about me. Or telling me what to do. I don't respond well. I've been independent for a very long time and that's just the way it is."

"I can testify to that. I'm independent myself."

"Yeah, I can see that. So…are we friends again?"

"Isn't that what friends do—tell the truth to each other, even when the other one doesn't want to hear it?" He hitched a brow.

She smiled. "You're right. Just don't get too bossy, buster." She laughed. "Things could get volatile."

"Yes, ma'am." Treb smiled finally.

Megan realized in that moment that her relationship with this man was going to be complicated…really complicated.

Treb opened the door for her and she moved past him into the hallway. She moved by him as quickly as possible, though she breathed in the scent of him as she brushed past him.

Betty rounded the corner and immediately started to fuss over her.

"You're back. Are you hurting? Do you need to sit down? What can I do for you?" The worried questions rolled out of the tiny spitfire faster than App's sunflower seeds hitting his spittoon.

"I'm fine. And like I told Treb, I don't need or want to be coddled."

Betty stuffed her hands on her hips. "Well fine. Suit yourself. But I've waited on you to get back here and I plan to coddle if I want to. It's six o'clock. Time for you to go home. I've alerted tomorrow's patients that you might not be in and Susan also knows what happened and is in agreement that you should take the day off."

"You worried Susan? She doesn't need to be worried. She has a newborn—"

"Relax, will you? I didn't tell her. She heard it through the grapevine."

"What grapevine? I didn't tell anyone."

Betty dropped her chin to her chest and gave her an are-you-kidding-me glare.

"She heard it from that good-looking hubby of hers. He heard it down at the diner from App and Stanley. Those two hard-a-hearing old coots hear everything they want to hear. Someone must have come in the diner and known about you and the stallion doing the tango."

"Who?"

Treb looked thoughtful. "I told Rafe. I had to let them know I wasn't going to be at the roundup. Maybe he or one of the other fellas said something about it at the diner."

"That's probably what it was," Betty said. "And if App and Stanley mentioned it once, they'd probably mentioned it to everyone who came in and listened."

Megan groaned. "Small-town life. Gotta love it.

Betty, make the calls and give tomorrow's appointments their slots back. I can work."

Betty frowned. "Fine. Stubborn woman…" she muttered as she headed back to the front desk. She spun and looked at Treb. "Thanks for rescuing her."

"My pleasure," he said to Betty and held Megan's gaze with his. "Let's just not make a habit of it."

She frowned at him and was glad when Betty went back to work. "Thank you for all you did but I'm sure you need to get back to work too."

He had his hand on the door and studied her. Something about the way his gaze lingered on her sent her pulse skittering.

"I'm going. But I came here for a reason this afternoon and I figure before I walk out the door, I need to finish what I came for. I know your leg might be a problem now but I came to ask you to go to the dance with me this weekend."

"The dance." She'd seen the flyers and had heard mention of the dance but she didn't dance much. "I'm actually a really bad dancer."

"I don't care."

"I'm not sure that's a good idea."

He cocked his head. "I don't bite."

Butterflies the size of Applegate's buzzard erupted inside her chest. "I don't—"

He suddenly was beside her and cupped her jaw with his hand. "Don't be afraid of me, Megan."

Her breath stuck in her lungs. "That's harder than you know," she managed.

"Then take it as a challenge. Say yes, Megan."

She tried to ignore the heat of his large palm. Tried to fight the lure of his words and of his gorgeous eyes…

And found it useless as very slowly she nodded.

He smiled. "Great. Now I'll get out of your way." And with that, he turned and walked out the door.

She didn't move.

"That is one hunky charmer right there," Betty said from behind her.

Megan jumped. Her stomach was tied in knots and the butterflies were everywhere.

She had just accepted another date with Treb. But this one would be in public.

At a dance. What had she been thinking?

She hadn't been. And that was his fault. He'd been so gentle, funny...nice. And bossy.

Drat the man. She wanted him to be hardheaded as he'd been when he'd jumped on her case but even then he'd explained that it had been done because he cared. All that together made him hard to resist.

Megan sighed. "You're right. But I'm not on the market, so this doesn't make sense."

"Not on the market? Girl, what kind of nonsense is that? You're young and got your life spread out ahead of you. Stop putting limitations on that life. You're supposed to get married. Make love, make babies, and enjoy the life you've been blessed with. And may I be the first to tell you that there is more to life than work."

Megan turned to Betty. "I enjoy my life, thank you very much. I don't have to get married to do that. But, just in case you didn't hear, I'm going to the dance Saturday night with him."

"Hallelujah!" Betty did a little dance of her own in the hallway with her hands lifted in the air.

"That's all there is to it, though. I'm just going to a

dance."

Betty halted. "Humph." She snorted. "I want to be a fly on your shoulder and see how long that lasts when that hunk of burnin' love puts his arms around you and y'all start swayin' to the music."

To emphasize her words, Betty started to sway and shot her a wink and then two-stepped her way back down the hallway and around the corner.

The truth lingered in the hallway behind Betty...Megan was in so much trouble and she knew it.

# CHAPTER EIGHT

Treb had thought of Megan ever since he'd left her at the clinic the day she'd been hurt. He wanted more than anything to check on her before Saturday but he hadn't wanted to give her the chance to cancel on him and he wasn't completely certain she wouldn't do it. He'd forced himself to stay away and every time his phone rang, he feared it would be her canceling.

But all that aside, he was excited to see her. Wanted to see how she was doing and he just wanted to be in her company. Something about her drove him crazy. He literally wanted to know her better. He knocked on the door and waited for her to open it.

Finally the door swung open. She took his breath right out of his chest.

Blew the barn doors off the building—she was a sight to behold in her sleeveless red dress.

"Wow." His gaze ran down her red dress to her fancy scrolled, Western boots and then back up to her beautiful face. "You are a sight to behold."

She laughed. "Flattery will not get you anywhere. Just so you know."

"Who's talking flattery? I'm just stating the facts."

She laughed again and he was hooked and hopeless.

Within moments, they were driving toward town. And he was lighthearted as he drove. They discussed her week, how her leg and hand were doing better and they discussed the weather. All the while, he struggled not to stare as his mind reeled with how glad he was to be with her again.

She could have worn a clown outfit and he would have been just as happy…well, maybe that was stretching it because he really liked her dress, but man oh man did he have to fight to focus on the road.

"So fill me in on the matchmakin' posse," she said, when they were halfway to town.

"Norma Sue, Esther Mae, and Adela?"

"Yes," she said. "I haven't been around them a lot. That's partly because I've been too busy to be around most everyone since coming to town. But I did happen to be at the diner when I first came to town and they kind of gave me the third degree. They didn't even try to hide their motives."

"Oh, they're pretty focused on their mission."

"To make sure everyone is married."

He smiled at her. "Yes, but it's to keep Mule Hollow alive. And they've secured our little town's future through helping cowboys find love."

"So that's it."

He nodded. "In a nutshell."

Megan was silent for a minute. "Will they be here tonight?"

"In full force. So I hope you're prepared for excessive scrutiny."

"Not really but I guess I don't have a choice."

"It'll be okay. The ladies take this very seriously so, maybe they'll be focused on others and miss us." He didn't believe that for a minute but he wanted to ease her mind if he could.

"That would be good. So do all the cowboys want to get married?"

"No. But, there are plenty who work long hours and just have trouble getting all the way to Ranger or other bigger towns to meet women. They're ready to settle down but it's just hard finding that right person when you're also working hard. They're all for these social events."

Megan looked thoughtful. "I can see why. What the ladies are doing makes sense."

"It does," he agreed. "All the partners of the New Horizon Ranch had a little help by them."

"Really?"

"Yes." He glanced at her in time to catch the surprised look on her face.

"Wow. They look like they are all-over-the-moon happy and in love."

"Oh, they are."

She looked thoughtful. "I'm in the same boat...*if* I were looking for a serious relationship, I'd hardly have time to seek it out. But I'm *not* looking. I'm happy just the way my life is right now. But what about you? I get that feeling that you're ready to settle down."

He wasn't going to lie. "I've seen a lot in my life...and I am ready. I want to share my life with someone; I want to fall in love and have kids-the whole package. My poor mother is so ready for grandkids. I want to give them to her. My brother was engaged when we lost him. And that tore her up. Then she's fought cancer over the last year and survived, and I'm ready to make her smile again at this time of her life."

"That's tough. I'm so glad she's survived."

"Me too."

"So why are you wasting your time with me?"

Her blunt question should have made him falter. Why *was* he wasting his time with someone who clearly wasn't looking to settle down? It was a good question.

He parked on the outskirts of town, where cars

started to line up. He cut the engine and turned his full attention to her. Her gorgeous golden eyes bore into him.

"Because to be quite blunt, I can't help myself." The flare of shock in every facet of her expression almost made him smile.

But he wasn't joking. Where she was concerned, he'd come to realize that he had no control over his emotions. He craved to be near her and no matter how much he wanted to give his mother the grandkids she deserved, right now none of that mattered.

# CHAPTER NINE

Megan stared at Treb. Her throat had gone dry and her mind fuddled at the look in his eyes and the truth in his tone...all making her believe his words...*I can't help myself.*

She'd had similar thoughts where he was concerned and now his words hung in the air, reverberating with the look in his eyes. He'd meant what he said.

This man—this gorgeous, shockingly, kind man who wanted a family and children—couldn't help himself when it came to her. A tingly feeling of warmth spread through her at the thought.

Did he have his eyes on her to fulfill this sweet family affair?

Or was she just a distraction, *a stop-off on his way to finding the woman of his dreams?*

She wasn't interested in marriage, so why did that thought settle like a lump in her stomach?

Her heart fought to believe the less-than-sweet version wasn't true. And why did she care? She wasn't interested.

As they got out of the truck, it dawned on her that there was another option…he wanted to mold her into this wife he had his cap set on. That thought caused her mouth to go dry.

"I'm not moldable," she blurted, startling herself.

That slightly crooked smile lifted engagingly. "I'm not looking to do any molding. Well, not a lot anyway. That mouth of yours I'd really like to mold to mine right now."

She gasped. "You are unrepentant."

"Is that what you call it? My brother used to call it something with a slightly less nice sound."

She laughed at that too. And he stepped close, as if he was going to do exactly what he'd said... Her heart thundered at the thought.

Lifting his hand, he ran his fingers lightly along her jaw. "Let's go dance," he said, his voice husky. And then he stepped back and waited for her to walk down the long stretch of pavement toward town.

Turmoil roiled inside her like a billowing wind before a tornado as they passed the line of vehicles parked along the side of the road.

The music could be heard in the distance. They were about to pass a cherry-red Jeep parked along the road when the door opened. A small woman swung her high-heeled feet to the grass and popped out of the vehicle.

"Treb," she called, beaming a bright smile his way. She was pretty, with short, mahogany hair that accented her huge eyes and high cheekbones. She took a step away from the car and her ankles wobbled as the high heels sank into the uneven ground. "Oops!" she exclaimed.

Treb reached for her. "Sugar Rae, let me help."

"Oh fiddles, thanks," she gasped and clutched his hand. She held on tight as she tottered the last step from the grass to the pavement. Once on smooth ground, she blew out a breath and chuckled. "I thought I was toast there for a moment. These shoes were not made for grass. What was I thinking?"

Treb let go of her hand but Megan could tell he was still on alert in case he had to steady the beauty again. "Are you steady now?"

"Yep. Thanks bunches. I wouldn't have liked a twisted ankle. I was planning on looking you up tonight. I've located a property you're going to want to look at. It's a real steal and it has everything you've specified on it. You might have to have an open mind where the house is concerned but you're really going to want to look at it soon. It won't last long."

"No kidding?" He looked excited. "I'm ready."

Looking at Sugar Rae's leopard print blouse and straight-legged black jeans rolled up at her ankles, paired with the mile-high heels—that she actually showed real estate in—had Megan rethinking her wardrobe. Maybe she needed an update. *Ridiculous*, she scolded herself.

Ridiculous was exactly how she'd look if she had that outfit on.

Treb would look at her as if she had lost her marbles if she had that outfit on...unlike the adoring way he looked at Sugar Rae.

The pretty woman continued, full of enthusiasm. "It's an awesome place and I think you're going to love it. I'll call you tomorrow and make a date to see it."

"I'll look forward to it."

"Great. Sounds like a plan." She smiled and then turned that mega-watt smile on Megan. "I'm sorry to ignore you. I was just so excited. I'm Sugar Rae Denton. I don't believe we've met."

"Oh, sorry," Treb interjected. "I assumed with all those animals you have that you'd been to the clinic and already met. This is Megan Tanner. She's taking slack for Susan while she's out on maternity leave."

"It's nice to meet you, Sugar Rae."

"Likewise. If you ever need some real estate, I'm at the office in town. I hate to run but I need to hurry.

My hubby is playing his little heart out up there with the band and I hate to miss too much more of it. You two enjoy the dance. And I'm sure we'll be meeting again since, as Treb said, I have a menagerie of animals out at my place." With that, she teetered off at a surprisingly fast pace on the hardtop.

Megan had been jealous. *Actually jealous…*

And Treb wasn't impressed by spiked heels.

The band was set up on a stage in the center of Main Street in front of the tiny town community center. She'd heard Betty say that it was decorated to the hilt and had all kinds of auction pieces inside for folks to bid on. The proceeds went to help the local women's shelter.

Treb led Megan through the crowd to the edge of the dance area. He was more than ready to get her on the dance floor and into his arms.

"I *heard* y'all were coming together!" Esther Mae Wilcox exclaimed, bursting through the crowd to get to them. "I am so excited!"

Treb groaned and hoped Megan didn't turn and march straight out of town with the way the red-haired matchmaker gaped at them.

"Esther Mae, it's just a date," Megan said, as if that would take the wind out of the redhead's sails.

"Of course it is. You're on a date with the man who saved you from getting stomped to death by a rampaging stallion. It's so romantic."

Megan's shocked gaze slung to Treb and he bit his lip to keep from smiling. One thing she'd have to learn was these women would see romance in everything.

"I'm glad Megan agreed to come with me," he said.

"I'm sure you are," Esther Mae cooed, and then suddenly waved wildly and looked past Megan. "Norma Sue, over here."

He didn't know whether Megan even realized that she stepped closer to him as Norma Sue in her white Stetson barreled through the crowd toward them.

"Don't panic," he said softly, so that only she could hear. "It's not that bad."

"Easy for you to say," she growled out the side of

her mouth. "I've heard the stories. I should have just said no."

He chuckled softly and had no plans to let this get in his way.

"Howdy, y'all," Norma Sue huffed as she careened to a halt in front of them. "I heard you were coming with Treb to the dance and I very nearly danced a jig. It's good for you to get out from behind all these pregnant cows and have a little fun finally. And Treb's been needing someone like you to come into town and light a spark in those pretty blue eyes of his."

She'd done that for certain. He winked at Megan; she narrowed her eyes and stomped his foot. He grunted and fell more in love with her spunk.


Megan forced a smile at the ladies and told herself to act normal. "I thought I'd come see the town kickin' up its feet," she said, deciding it was best not to comment on Treb's beautiful eyes.

"Oh, it can do that," Esther Mae gushed. "And you

needed some time to do the same. All work and no play isn't good for anyone."

"That's so true," Treb said and she almost elbowed him. She did not need him to say anything that would encourage the ladies by him sounding as though he approved of their schemes.

"And dancing is a good way to do it." Norma Sue's grin grew wider.

Both women eyed Megan as if she were under a microscope. She tried not to squirm and gave a halfhearted smile.

She had no one to blame for this but herself. She'd known this was going to happen. That going to the dance with Treb would alert the posse that there was a potential love match in the air. Not true, but still she had set herself up for this.

Esther Mae leaned toward her and said, almost conspiratorially, "I tell you, we've had our eye on this cowboy and we keep trying to find him a match but have just not come up with a candidate. Until you."

Treb cleared his throat. "Esther Mae, I'm standing right here. And you and the ladies will be sad to know that Megan is not on the market."

"What do you mean?" Norma Sue barked. "Do not tell me you are not interested in falling in love? Look at you."

"Yes, look." Esther Mae looked distressed.

The band that was tightening around her windpipes yanked tight. "It's okay to be single," she said defensively.

Treb chuckled beside her. "Yes, it is. Ladies, it's been nice but I think Megan's ready to dance." And suddenly he swept her into his arms and gently pulled her out into the street to join the other dancers.

Over his shoulder, she saw the two women looking as if they'd just won the lottery or something as they watched Treb dance her away from them.

"Why did you do that?" she hissed, turning her head up to glare at him.

He just grinned down at her. "Do what? We came to dance, didn't we?"

"Yes, but now they'll really talk," she growled, but found herself distracted by the feel of his hard chest beneath her forearm. Her hand might be in a cast but the exposed part of her arm that was crammed between her and his chest could feel every hard inch of muscled chest.

He squeezed her good hand in his and then intertwined their fingers. "Darlin', they're going to talk no matter what you or I want," he said, against her ear.

She shivered at the warmth of his breath against her skin.

"This was a bad idea." She tried to hold her voice steady.

He pulled his head back so he could look at her. "There was nothing about this that was a bad idea. At least not for me." He pulled her close and led her into a slow two-step deeper into the crowd.

Her heart galloped, making it hard to concentrate on anything but him. She was in his arms and he was holding her so close…and he smelled unbelievably good—so good.

The only concentration she was doing was on how to keep herself from laying her head on his shoulder and wrapping her arms tightly around him.

And never letting go.

She panicked on that thought. When the dance ended, she pushed away from him—it was a protective reaction. Staying in his arms was not safe for her right now. But Treb didn't let go of her hand and the band barely paused from the end of one song before moving straight into the new song. Treb smiled sexily, shot her a wink and then tugged her back into his arms, spinning with her in several fast circles to the beat of the music as couples all around them broke out into the jitterbug.

Startled by the move, laughter bubbled out of her as Treb spun them to the rhythm of the jitterbug tune. At last he stopped spinning and held her steady as the world stopped whirling around them. Breathless and totally exhilarated, she looked up at him.

"That smile is a good thing to see." His voice turned husky and for a moment she thought he was going to kiss her there in front of the whole world.

She tensed.

His smile faded and his expression grew somber. "Relax, Megan. Just enjoy the night. If you're worried about the posse, please don't. You can't control what those three enthusiastic ladies think or do. Or anyone else, for that matter." He began to lead them to the music again.

*Relax.* Easy for him to say. She felt a sense of alarm—this man was a danger to her plans.

A danger to her long-ago decision to remain alone. If he kept this up, she knew she was going to fall hard for him. And she just couldn't do it.

# CHAPTER TEN

When the second song ended, Treb forced himself to let her go. "Do you want to grab a drink? I saw a refreshment stand earlier."

"That sounds wonderful."

The posse was now all lined up behind the refreshment stand. Including Adela. The sweet lady's face lit up with welcome as they halted in front of the booth.

"What a blessing it is to see the two of you enjoying the evening so much," she said with a gentle warmth to her words. Her vibrant blue eyes stood out in contrast to her silky cap of white hair. Something about Sam's wife made everyone feel comfortable and special. She was also the calming voice, he suspected, in the midst of the overwhelming enthusiasm of her two cohorts.

"Hi, Adela. It's nice to see you. I have to tell you that I adore your sweet husband. I've been so busy I'd have starved if it wasn't for him and his diner."

"He loves every minute of it. And I adore him too. Treb, you are looking so handsome tonight. You clean up real nice."

Treb chuckled. "Well, thank you, ma'am. I try real hard to impress."

Esther Mae leaned forward over the table and sniffed. "And you smell plumb edible. My Hank needs some of that foo-foo you're wearing."

"I've got to smell that." Norma Sue slapped her hands on the table and leaned forward. Being shorter than Esther Mae, she had to stretch farther and put more weight on the table. "Hot dog, you do smell good. Megan, you must be in heaven dancing with him."

Treb laughed just as the table buckled beneath the ladies. Cups, plastic pitchers of lemonade, Esther Mae, and Norma Sue all crashed to the ground. Norma Sue landed on the ground with Esther Mae on top.

"Holy smokes! Get your elbow out of my ribs, Esther!" Norma Sue yelled.

"I'm trying. Please get your knee out of my hip!"

"I'm trying but…"

Treb had moved to help and grabbed for their flailing arms. He got one of each and held on.

"Let me help too." Megan reached in and took Esther Mae's other arm with her hand that didn't have a cast on it. The redhead's hair was drenched in sticky lemonade and she was blinking through trickles weaving down her face. Instead of tears like Megan expected, she was chuckling so hard her shoulders shook.

Below her, Norma Sue was flat on her back, her white Stetson halfway over her face. Lemonade puddled in the rim of the hat. She reached up with her free hand and took the hat off her face. All the lemonade poured from the rim and splattered directly in her face.

She sputtered. "Adela! Your lemonade is as good as always," she called out, and then busted out laughing.

A crowd had gathered and among them was Rafe and Dalton. Treb was glad to see them.

"Let us help you get them up," Rafe said to him.

"Ladies, can you move okay?" Dalton moved to the other side of the table to help from that angle.

"Yes." Esther Mae chuckled again. "Although Norma Sue was a nice padding for me. She's the one who hit the ground."

"I'm fine. Except I think I'm lying on a ladle and that's gonna be one funny bruise on my backside."

Treb helped Dalton get Esther Mae up and then reached to help Rafe get Norma Sue off the ladle and to her feet.

Adela immediately went to wiping the wetness off their faces. "You two scared me," she said. "Come on. Let's go get y'all into the diner and cleaned up."

Their husbands arrived, hustling up to help.

"Esther honey, what have you two been up to?"

Hank Wilcox gently took her by the elbow.

Esther Mae grinned. "Just helping with the excitement."

Treb shook his head. "Y'all scared ten years off my life. I think I can do without that kind of excitement from here on out."

Esther Mae just laughed and let Hank lead her toward the diner.

"You two can get into more mischief. You sure you're okay?" Roy Don asked Norma Sue.

She grinned. "I'm fine and probably sweeter than I've ever been in my life since I'm wearing Adela's lemonade all over me." She shot Treb a grin. "Don't slow down. Y'all get back out there and kick up your heels…just not like me and Esther just did."

That got a round of laughter as the ladies disappeared into the diner.

Megan sighed as the crowd dispersed. "They scared me half to death."

"Me too." He wiped a splotch of liquid from her cheek. "You're going to be a little sticky yourself."

Her eyes twinkled. "I'll live. At least now that

they're not hurt."

"Ahem." Rafe cleared his throat loudly and Treb remembered his bosses were standing beside him.

"Thanks for y'alls help." He turned his attention to Rafe and Dalton.

Dalton straightened his hat and hitched his brows. "I didn't realize you even knew we were here."

"That's the truth," Rafe agreed.

Treb glanced at Megan. "Well, there was a lot going on and Megan's a whole heap better looking than you two."

Ty walked up with Mia in tow. "That's the honest truth." He smiled at Megan. "I'm Ty," he said. "And this is my wife Mia."

"It's great to meet you. Maddie has told us you're a wonderful vet. She said you really look after her orphans. And that says a lot since she adores her baby calves."

"I love them too. She does a fantastic job getting the nurse mamas to take them on."

"Thanks." Maddie joined the growing group. "I try. There's a soft spot in my heart for the little darlings."

"I'm Cliff," a handsome cowboy said. He looked slightly familiar but she couldn't figure out why. "I'm also Rafe's twin, but we don't look alike."

"It's nice to meet you all." Megan looked around the group and then stopped back on Cliff. "I knew you looked familiar and I see now you and Rafe resemble each other. But I'd have never thought y'all were twins."

Rafe leaned forward and winked. "I'm the pretty one."

Cliff grunted. "You got that right. I don't want anyone calling me pretty."

Maddie wrapped her arms around him. "I think you are."

His scowl was comical. "Woman, you're the pretty one in this twosome. I'm just grateful you love an ugly cowboy like me."

Maddie cocked her head at everyone. "He sure can get ornery, can't he?"

Chase leaned in and held out his hand. "May be time for a subject change. Y'all are freaking me out with all the pretty talk. I'm Chase, the other partner of the ranch. My wife is inside helping with the auction. Thanks for saving our cow and calf the other night."

"Nice to meet you and you're welcome. Just doing my job."

"Treb told us you were amazing." Maddie grinned. "But I already knew that."

"Amazing, huh?" She laughed but felt a nice little squeeze of her heart knowing he'd said she was amazing.

"You were," he said.

"Thanks." She bent and picked up several cups. Everyone else started doing the same. The men moved the broken table out of the way. Everyone chatted and teased and Megan found herself enjoying herself with Treb's friends.

When they were all done, Chase left to go see his wife, promising to introduce her later. Then Ty and Mia went off to dance and Rafe's wife Sadie showed up and was shocked to know what had happened. She'd been inside working the auction too.

"I leave y'all for a few minutes and you get into trouble," Sadie teased as Rafe moved behind her and slipped his arms around her.

"That's right." He snuggled her close to him. Sadie leaned her head back on his shoulder. He kissed her gently on the temple. "So you shouldn't leave me alone. I'm glad you showed up. I was feeling lonesome."

Sadie turned her head to him and gave him a gentle kiss on the lips. "Sorry about that."

"Are you ready to dance?" he asked her and Megan got the feeling that they were locked in a world of their own in that moment.

"I thought you'd never ask."

He shifted so that he was beside Sadie with one arm draped over her shoulder. "Excuse us. We've got some catching up to do."

Megan smiled. "Have fun."

"Nice to meet you again," Sadie said and then let her husband lead her off to the crowded street, where dancing was in full swing.

Lost in thought, Megan watched them go.

"A penny for your thoughts," Treb said, coming from where he'd been fixing them glasses of tea from the refreshment tables that hadn't bit the dust. He handed her a red cup filled with iced-down sweet tea.

She took a long drink. It felt so good as it slid down her dry throat.

"I'll give you two pennies to know what's going on behind those beautiful eyes of yours."

"I was just thinking about how happy and in love all your bosses seem."

"Yeah, it's cool, isn't it?"

She nodded. "It is...I—" Thoughts of her sisters' failed marriages and of her mom's many jumbled in her mind. "I just don't think I could ever..."

"Ever what? Marry?" He studied her with eyes that seemed to look straight to her soul.

She shook her head. "Nothing. It's..." Her words trailed off. She wasn't ready to let anyone see how much she feared failure. Feared wanting something with all of her heart and then seeing it slip away...slip through her fingertips.

"It is something," Treb said, so gently that her heart clenched in reaction. "I can't help but feel something deep is going on inside that pretty head and sweet heart of yours."

She blinked sudden tears away. *What was wrong*

*with her?* She sniffed. "Let's dance." She started toward the music.

"Whoa, hold on," Treb urged and moved to block her path. "Talk to me. Don't leave me hanging."

She'd halted and now she tried to sidestep him. "I can't. I want to dance."

He held her gaze for a moment and then gave her that grin she was quickly coming to love. "If the lady wants to dance, then the lady gets to dance."

She did want to dance and there was no denying it. She was here to have fun and that didn't mean she had to get married. She'd told Betty that and she'd meant it. Thinking any other way than that was too dangerous for her.

Treb hooked an arm around her and took her broken hand gently, holding it close to his heart as he danced them back out into the crowd.

And Megan's heart thundered louder than the music, pounding out a love song all its own.

The moon illuminated the road as Treb headed from the dance toward Megan's house. She had a huge dilemma on her hands. She didn't want the night to end.

Treb cocked his head to look at her halfway to her house. "I had another great night, Megan."

"I did too." She was going to have to decide whether to ask him to come inside when they reached her house...but she was actually afraid of herself right now. She had never felt so drawn to a man, so overwhelmed by the feelings that his touch evoked in her. And she'd been in his arms for most of the night, dancing and having the time of her life. But there had been a crowd around them and she had been very aware that Norma Sue and Esther Mae had returned to the dance and were grinning and watching them like a hawk.

Thoughts of the posse had kept her from allowing her head to rest on his shoulder or from giving in to the want to snuggle closer to him. But the posse wasn't here now and she could lay her head on his shoulder if she wanted to.

"I'm going to check hog traps after I drop you off...you wouldn't want to come, would you?"

*Hog hunting?* Megan's eyes narrowed in reflex and surprise at the unexpected statement.

"I know you're probably tired and this is an odd request, but I don't want the night to end...and I know when I walk you to your door, you'll disappear into your house and it will end."

*He was thinking exactly what she was thinking.* "I'd love to go check traps with you." She found she liked the idea of spending some alone time with him...without the watchful eyes of the whole town. And there were the warm thoughts of his lips on hers that had her pulse kicking into flight at the possibility.

He was watching the road again and now met her gaze with a grin that seemed to sparkle in the light of the dashboard. "You're sure? Maybe we can talk while we're out there. I'd like very much to spend some time alone with you and not in a crowd."

*Talk?* Not exactly where her thoughts had gone. "Sure," she said, but felt a little trepidation sneak into the night.

# CHAPTER ELEVEN

*Checking hog traps? What was he thinking?*

That he was desperate to keep her with him longer tonight.

That he didn't want the night to end because he wanted to spend time with her.

All true...but most of all, he was obsessed with finding out what had happened at the dance when she'd lost herself in her thoughts and had looked so heart wrenchingly lost there for a few minutes. Something deep was affecting Megan and he needed to know what it was.

He'd danced with her and thoroughly enjoyed himself but he wanted to know what she was feeling in her heart and why the idea of his bosses being so in love and happy had affected her the way that it had.

But seriously—*checking hog traps?* Surely there could have been a better excuse to extend the night but that was all he could think of when it came down to the wire. And she'd surprised him when she'd said yes instead of laughing at him and saying, "Take me home, cowboy."

And here they were, bumping along the countryside beneath a gorgeous moon.

He shot her a skeptical look. "Really, you want to go hog hunting?"

"Are you kidding?" she gasped and the trepidation that had been written on her face melted away. "As long as you're not going to whip out a gun and start shooting, then I'm in for some pasture time. The dance was fun, but a little tense with all the eyes that I felt were watching us. I can let my hair down and relax."

"Honey, I'm all in on you letting your hair down and relaxing."

She laughed in a bubbly, happy sound that twisted in his chest and reached into the dark space deep in his heart desperately needing some light. When he'd been in the field on missions in the dark of the night, his brother had been constantly on his mind. He'd grieved in the field and his heart had hardened around that grief. He'd been angry at God during that time. When he'd needed God the most, Treb had been too angry to seek him out. But despite everything, God had never let go of him and He'd brought Treb home safe…and physically unscathed. For that he was grateful. And eventually he'd turned back to the Lord and embraced the grace that had been shown him during that dark time. But now he wanted more…he wanted a future and he'd found it in the beautiful woman sitting in the truck with him.

He'd been falling in love with Megan from their first meeting. And tonight he knew he wanted her in his life. He wanted to know her story and felt there was a pain there that he wanted to try to help heal.

He needed the light of love in his life. Love was the healer and he couldn't help feel as though whatever troubled Megan could be healed by love too.

He reached the barn and parked and hopped from the truck. She climbed out before he got around to open her door for her.

She glanced around. "What are we doing here?"

He nodded to the all-terrain vehicle that sat inside the barn. "Thought we'd take the Gator into the bogs where I've set the traps. And since the night is so nice…"

Her smile flashed. "Oh, cool. I wish I had on my jeans and boots and I'd get to really be a country girl."

"I understand your thinking but you do look really pretty in that dress. I will not lie."

She laughed. "I do enjoy wearing them sometimes. Since a dress is impractical for work."

"Yeah, I could see where that could be a problem."

They were laughing as they climbed into the ATV and headed toward the creek. The ATV wasn't big and she was much closer to him now than when they'd been in his truck. He liked that. If she hadn't been wearing that dress, he'd have opted for the four-wheeler and the opportunity to have her arms wrapped around him and the feel of her close to him as they traveled through the night.

As it was, he was just glad to have her near him.

Megan's hair ruffled around her as Treb drove them across the pasture. The feel of the wind was exhilarating at the fast clip that he drove. All other thoughts melted away and she just let herself enjoy the moment.

"Hold on." He started down the steep incline. "We're heading to the creek bed."

"Fun!" she called over the growl of the engine. "I so needed this."

"I did too," he said and his smile warmed her heart and she got a glimpse of the teenager he'd once been. "I love being outside." He shot her that glance of his that caused her stomach to wobble.

"I love it outside too."

"I get that about you."

And that was the thing about him that touched her deeply—he got her. He seemed to really understand what drove her, even when she wasn't speaking. At the dance earlier, he'd wanted to know what was bothering her; he'd known something was and yet he'd pulled back when she'd said she didn't want to talk about it. So instead of pushing her, he'd listened to her and swept her into his arms and they'd danced the night away.

His pulling back had given her time to think. Time to wonder whether maybe speaking to him about her fears might be a good thing. But she'd never opened up to anyone about why she wasn't going to ever marry. And she wasn't sure she could.

Water splashed as Treb drove the ATV across the shallow creek and then up the other embankment and along the rim on his way to one of the large cages that was a trap for the hogs.

"Look at that," Megan gasped when she saw how terrible the ground was torn up. Deep ruts and holes riddled the moonlit landscape. "This is terrible."

"Yeah," he called over the engine. "And it's only

the beginning." As he drove, the full moon exposed the destruction further. "This is one of the hay pastures. We'll have to come in and smooth all this out before we can plant hay again. And they've destroyed a lot of hay that was ready to cut and bale. The hay baling equipment won't be able to get over this rough ground, so they'll just have to lose it."

He hit an unexpectedly deep rut and it threw them both into the air. Megan was thrown forward and Treb grabbed her around the waist before she could get tossed out of the vehicle. She grabbed for him too and landed back in the bench seat much closer to him than she had been.

She was laughing when he brought the Gator to a jarring halt. The pure joy of her laughter settled into him like a ball of sunshine.

"Are you alright?" He was amazed at the emotions her laughter evoked in him.

"I'm fine. I was just looking somewhere else when you hit that ginormous rut. I wasn't holding onto anything. Now we know that I bounce like a rubber ball."

He laughed at that. "You've definitely got some bounce. I think I'll be more careful. If I hit another one like that, you could be thrown out or the axle of the Gator could break and we'd be walking out of here."

She lifted a booted foot. "I've got my boots on tonight so it'd be no problem."

That made him smile more and the sun she'd brought into his life intensified. "Do you know how many women would think that was a horrible idea on a dark night like tonight?"

"Dark? The moon has it lit up like Vegas."

Treb cut the engine and the silence of the night surrounded them. "Megan." Unable to stop himself, he slid his hand beneath her silky hair and cupped her neck as he drew her the last few inches closer to him. She came willingly, her eyes never leaving his and as she lifted her face to his, he kissed her.

It seemed as if he'd been waiting a lifetime for this next kiss and he'd have waited longer if he'd had to…he'd wait a lifetime if he needed to.

Megan's lips were welcoming and warm as he deepened the kiss. He had to fight to contain the passion that built through him just holding her. No one had ever pushed him to the near breaking point.

"Do you know how rare you are?" he said against her lips.

She pulled away and touched his cheek with her hand. That look he'd seen earlier came over her and she pulled away.

"Treb—"

"Megan, what are you thinking when you turn so serious and so sad?" His gut clenched looking at her.

Her brows knit. "What do you mean?" she asked so softly he almost didn't hear.

"Don't try to deny that something important isn't going on behind those beautiful eyes of yours. I want to help. You can talk to me."

She sighed and just looked at him with shadowed eyes that cut through him.

He got out of the vehicle and, holding her hand, he drew her with him. He needed the freedom to wrap his arms completely around her. "Talk to me, Megan, because I have to tell you that I've fallen fast and hard for you. And I know that may scare you off but I'm there. However, you're in control at this point."

He felt her heart thunder against his, felt her stiffen against him at his declaration. He realized he might have made a huge mistake but it was what it was...every fiber of his body and soul was hers. There was no turning back for him now.

"Treb, I can't do this." Megan hid her face against Treb's shoulder as fear rocked through her. "This is too deep."

She'd been longing all night to rest her head on his shoulder, to feel his arms around her while he kissed her. To feel as if it were just them and nothing else mattered...even though she knew it did. For just this minute, she could imagine that in this one perfect moment she had it all.

"Too deep for what, honey?"

Tears threatened at his endearment. He'd been doing it all night and each time her heart smiled. "I'm not what you need. I can't—"

"Can't what? Talk to me."

She didn't want to pull away but she forced herself to put space between them. However, looking at him didn't make it any easier. He was too gorgeous and too willing to be hers.

"I'm not the marrying kind. I told you...I watched my mother serial date all my life. I never knew who my dad was because he left us so early. She tried to believe in love and married a few times but nothing has ever lasted. And then, both my sisters hung on and believed in happily-ever-afters and both of those marriages have fallen apart. Love...love is just too hard. Both of them are devastated by the loss of their marriages. I just don't want to go there."

She saw his expression turn almost curious. "I'm sorry for their pain but I can't do anything about that except wish them happiness one day soon. I'm in love with you and you're saying you don't want to fall in love?"

"I told you from the beginning that I don't want to get married."

"Or fall in love?"

"That's what I'm saying. Have been saying."

"Your expression at the dance said differently."

"You saw an expression and read what you wanted to into it."

"Maybe, but I believe I'm right. You said you're always honest. Be honest with me, Megan."

She glared at him. "Who are you to push me, or accuse me of not being honest?"

"I'm a man who cares for you."

She turned away and walked over the rough ground—very glad she had on her boots. Her good hand was clenched at her side and her gut was tied in a knot. *Who did he think he was?*

He tromped beside her. "Don't walk away from this, Megan."

"Stop telling me what to do." She spun and lost her balance; he reached out and grasped her arm to steady her. She yanked her arm free of him as panic clenched inside her. He was too close. Too close to the truth.

"Megan, I spent my time in Afghanistan. I lost my brother to a suicide bomber and he left behind a fiancée who to this day hasn't opened up to the possibility of falling in love again. My brother would hate that. The one thing I learned through that is that life is precious. And short. God gave me another shot at it and I can't look back any longer. I'm looking forward. Maybe you should try that. Stop living in the regrets and unhappy events of your mother and sisters and step out for your own happiness. Don't be afraid."

*Afraid.* She crossed her arms and tried to harden her heart against his words. "You've chosen what you want and I've chosen what I want. I don't want to go through the pain that I've seen my mom and sisters go through and that's okay."

His gaze softened in the moonlight. "You are afraid. Megan, don't be afraid of me. I'd never hurt you."

"My sisters believed that once. And my mom…countless times. It's just not a promise I can say yes to." She was completely startled by the look of confusion on his face.

"You really mean that, don't you?"

"Treb, you wanted the truth. I don't say anything I don't mean. And we haven't even known each other that long, so it's outlandish that we're even having this conversation."

"Outlandish," he repeated as he picked up a strand of her hair and rubbed it between his fingers. "You're telling me that you don't feel the connection with me that I feel with you?"

She couldn't lie and say no. There was no denying it even if she wanted to. It was too strong. "I do. But that doesn't mean I have to let it have control."

"You're afraid of losing control."

She sucked in a breath as his observation struck a chord inside her. "No—"

His brows lifted slightly; his forehead creased as she felt his silent challenge.

"There's nothing wrong with wanting to control...things." The last word came out totally without conviction and grated on her nerves.

"Where was your carefully constructed control on that first kiss we shared? Or the last kiss we shared?"

He stepped close and she was certain he could feel her heart pounding even though he wasn't touching her. "Treb..." Her words trailed off as he leaned in and gently kissed her temple.

"Megan…" he softly said and then kissed her jaw.

Her pulse careened recklessly, as if she were sliding feet first down a slick slope leading to a cliff. She fought not to reach for him, to save herself from the precipice. She could not let her fears go, though. Could not chance the unknown.

*Love…*

The word echoed through her. Twisted in her chest and caused her heart to ache…like a deep well of tears that needed release. She'd longed for love for so long. But had never felt…*it. This…*

Treb cupped her face and tenderly kissed her forehead. And each kiss threatened to tear a brick out of the wall around her heart.

Suddenly, he stepped back and his expression wrenched at her aching heart.

"I won't push you, Megan. I knew what I was getting myself into when I started falling for you. You told me early on you weren't looking for love. I heard you. I just didn't listen…so I think the blame for the dilemma that I find myself in is of my own creation.

Not yours."

She couldn't move. Couldn't speak. Her skin craved his touch. Her soul craved his nearness.

"I think it's time for me to take you home so you can get some sleep so you'll be ready for your week."

"But what about the traps?"

"We'll pass by them before we cut back over the creek."

"Oh." She managed to hold her voice steady. This was what she wanted. What she'd asked for. She'd built these walls and created these rules. And he was going to abide by them.

Oddly enough, that thought made her madder than the large hog they found snorting angrily inside the sturdy wire trap a few minutes later.

# CHAPTER TWELVE

"You've worked days and nights every day this week," Dalton said on Thursday afternoon. "I thought you had started dating Megan."

Treb squinted against the bright sunlight as sweat trickled down his spine. He slammed the posthole digger into the packed ground, and then worked the two handles back and forth as he dug out another shovel full of soil. He didn't speak until he'd released the dirt on top of the small pile to the left of the hole. "I took her to the dance. Everyone assumed we were dating."

"So, you're not going out with her again?" Dalton dropped the cedar post into the hole and Treb steadied it as Dalton picked up a shovel and filled dirt in around it.

"Megan's her own woman. She has her own way of thinking and getting too involved is not on the list." Treb ignored the way his gut twisted at the question and the knowing look in Dalton's eyes. He knew that anyone who'd watched them at that dance could tell that he was over the moon for Megan. He'd worn his feelings on his sleeve like a fool.

What had he been thinking? He'd fallen like a rockslide for her despite all her warnings. All her signs. He had no one to blame but himself.

"So you knew this when you asked her out? Or did you find this out on the date?"

"I knew already. She lays things out in the open pretty fast." And now that he'd laid his cards on the table with her, all he could do was wait.

"I see. Rae Anne had wondered why y'all didn't sit together at church Sunday."

He'd seen her at church and they'd been friendly,

like friends, nothing more. They'd not sat together, which should have been a clue to Dalton and the rest of the community that things were going well with him and Megan.

He'd been busy. He had ranch work to do and projects to oversee for the partners and then he'd volunteered to rebuild this broken fence when they could have had any one of the other ranch hands do it. But he'd wanted the release that physical exertion provided.

And then at night he'd trapped hogs and moved them to the pens where they'd await transport off the property. And in between that, he'd gone twice a day to feed and oversee Maddie's orphaned calves. To say he was busy was an understatement. But it helped him not give in to the need to see Megan. He was giving her space.

He was giving her control.

If that's what she needed, then that's what she'd get. He just hoped...no, he prayed she'd develop feelings for him.

If she didn't, then he was in trouble. His mom was

in trouble, too, because those grandchildren that she'd been wishing for were now a distant fleck on the horizon.

"She's her own person. She went out with me—"

"And you want more." Dalton stopped filling the hole and studied Treb.

"I cannot lie. I'd like a whole lot more. But it's early and we've had two dates."

"They say three's the charm."

Treb's lip hitched up on one side. "Are you a cowboy or a romantic?"

Dalton laughed. "Both these days. If you'd have asked me that before I rescued Rae Anne, I'd have said a flat no. But things change. And they can change quick, so keep holding the line."

"That's a given. I'm not going anywhere." And that was exactly what Megan didn't believe. She didn't believe a man could say he loved a woman and then stick around to prove it. At least not where she and her sisters and mom were concerned.

He'd like to kick a few fellas' butts right now for what they'd caused Megan to falsely believe. She had an error in thinking where men were concerned…and he was going to prove it to her, no matter how long it took.

Megan walked into Pete's Feed and Seed on Friday morning to pick up goat feed and dog food. Archie pranced beside her. He was thrilled that today he got to ride in the truck with her. It wasn't something she let him do a lot of but every once in a while it was a treat for him. He was well behaved and took commands readily but when she was working it was about other people's animals, not her own that she needed to fuss over.

"Hey, Pete, how's it going?"

"If it was any better, I'd feel guilty. How'r you doing?"

"I can't complain. Things were booming and now I have a little breathing room so I'm enjoying the break."

He chuckled. "When it rains, it pours."

He petted Archie on the head and then reached for

the can of dog biscuits that he kept near the register. Archie sat and wagged his tail the instant he sniffed the treat.

"He knows to sit even before I tell him to."

"He taught himself. I think he believes if he does it before asked that he'll get two treats."

Pete hooted with laughter and handed Archie a second treat. "Works for me. What can I get you?"

"The usual. My goats are growing and eating me out of everything."

"They'll do it. Does the golden one need some too?"

"No, he has plenty right now."

"I'll be right back."

Her phone rang as Pete disappeared through the swinging door into the feed area. A glance told her it was her mom.

"Hi, Mom." She instantly felt guilty because she hadn't called her in a while. If her mother got even a whiff that she'd been on a couple of dates...Megan might never hear the end of it. And there was no way she was telling her mom about Treb.

She was fighting to not think of him herself. And there were already plenty of folks in Mule Hollow who weren't going to let her forget him any time soon. It was beginning to feel as if she were caught in a revolving door and couldn't get out. The posse asked her about him every chance they got and lately it seemed she ran into the ladies far more than she used to.

"'Hi, Mom'? That's all I get after nothing for nearly three weeks. Are you alive out there? And please tell me you are not standing at the south end of a cow right now."

She bit back a smile. "No, Mom, I am not delivering a calf right now. I'm at the feed store. And I'm sorry I haven't called. How are you?"

"I'm fine. I'm getting counseling and I thought you'd want to know."

Shock did a donut in her chest. "Counseling. Why?"

"Well, George asked me to."

This was so very unlike her mother. "Why would George ask you to get counseling?"

There was a pause and then her mother let out a long sigh. "Because I asked him for a divorce."

*Here we go again.* "I know y'all have had your ups and downs in the two years you've been married but I thought you loved him. Why did you ask him for a divorce? Did he do something?"

"I have been happy and I haven't made it easy on the poor man. I've pushed him away whenever he's tried to get closer to me and I've just been so afraid I'd lose him that I ended up pushing him farther and farther away."

"But, Mom, you try so hard to make your marriages work."

"Yes, I did…but I was always afraid something would go wrong. George is so different than Dave or Paul. He really meant his vows." There was disbelief in her mother's voice.

"Isn't that the way it's supposed to work?"

"Yes, but it just hasn't worked out for me. I just kept believing that I could find the right man who would mean what he said but I don't think deep down inside that I believed I was worthy of a man really loving me. I was pushing George away in so many small ways and I didn't even realize it. So when he asked me to go to counseling with him, I panicked. And I asked him for a divorce. Then the most amazing thing happened. He told me that he wasn't giving up on us and that he was going to fight for our relationship."

Megan walked to the back of the store so she could try to talk privately as some cowboys came inside. The wonder and happiness in her mom's voice was clear.

"But I'm confused, Mom."

"I know you are, honey, and that's why I had to call. Listen to me. I know I've had my share of ups and downs and I've taken you and your sisters on the ride with me. And for that I'm sorry. I want you to find a man who will make you happy...but I have learned something in the last two weeks of counseling and it's that I have to be happy with who I am before I can find happiness with someone else. Does that make sense?"

At this point, Megan wasn't sure any of this made sense but she said yes anyway.

"Good. Because you need to be happy, honey."

"I am."

"Maybe. But I'll leave that to you to figure out. I've got enough on my plate making myself happy right now. And George. That man is kind of bossy when it comes to making me think good things about myself."

That made Megan smile. "I'm happy for you, Mom."

"Good. Now, George is waiting in the car and we're off to our afternoon session. Love you, honey."

Megan said good-bye. Lost in thought, she stared at the supply of horse liniment, not actually seeing it. She wasn't sure what exactly to think of the conversation. Her mother had always projected overbearing optimism despite her failed marriages. It had always frustrated Megan. Now to know—at least, she thought this was what her mother had been conveying—that she'd been afraid and in that fear, she'd pushed her husbands away or kept them at a distance, was startling.

It made sense, though.

The more Megan thought about it, the more sense it made.

But that had nothing to do with her.

*Nothing.*

She walked back up front. Archie pranced beside her as she signed the invoice Pete had waiting for her while she continued to mull over her mother's revelation.

"Give me a minute and I'll load that for you," Pete said from where he was showing a cowboy something at the end of the counter.

"That's okay. I've got this." She leaned down a bit and then shouldered the fifty-pound bag and steadied it with both her good hand and her casted hand.

"No you don't," a deep voice said from behind her.

Treb took the bag from her shoulders and frowned at her. "Do you want to hurt yourself more?"

Archie wiggled from one end of his body to the other in happiness as he gazed up at Treb.

Megan knew how Archie felt and ignored the leap of joy she felt at seeing Treb. "Thank you." She turned and headed out the door. He followed her to her truck and placed the fifty-pound bag in the bed. She was very aware of him and tried to not let her emotions show in her expression. *He'd said he loved her.*

Words that she'd lived with for days now. Words she just wasn't sure what to do with.

"Thank you." She forced herself to look him in the eyes. *Oh, that was dangerous.*

Those blue eyes crinkled at the edges as his lips lifted into a gentle smile. "How are you?" He leaned against her truck and patted his stomach. Instantly, Archie rose on his hind legs and placed his front paws on Treb's taut stomach. Treb grinned at the dog and grasped both of Archie's ears affectionately.

Megan groaned silently and tried to seem unaffected. But it was hard. "I'm fine. Susan's back part-time and so that helps. Plus, as you know, the fields are full of baby calves and so that eases up the job."

"They're everywhere, that's for certain." He'd been looking at Archie and now cocked his head and shot that grin of his at her.

It was like an arrow straight to her heart. "How are you doing?" she asked.

"Missing you."

Her mouth went dry. "Not fair."

"Never said I was going to play fair. So just because I'm not trailing you around all the time, don't think you're not on my mind."

"You…" she started; then, her thought lost, she looked at the ground. "I need to go."

"Megan, come on. I was just teasing." Treb pushed away from the truck.

She pulled her door open. "Archie, load up." Archie just looked at her and then at Treb. "Archie." He flopped his tail on the ground.

"If I promise to behave, will you go out with me?"

"No."

He held his hands up in surrender and stepped back. "Okay, I get it. Load up, Archie," he said and her dog jumped into the truck.

Exasperated, Megan followed and slammed the door. Treb lowered his hands and placed them on his hips…and said nothing as she turned the key and the engine came to life. Megan felt as if the truck sat on her chest instead of her sitting in the driver's seat. Her mouth felt like cotton and her palms felt clammy as she clutched the steering wheel. "Look, Treb. I'll admit that there is something between us."

He nodded but didn't move from where he stood.

"But you need to let it go. At least for now. Meetings like this are just going to cause problems."

He strode to her door then and placed his hand on the window. "You are the most stubborn woman I've ever met."

"And you're the most stubborn man I've ever met. Just because you told me that you love me does not mean I have to reciprocate."

"But you do."

Her mouth dropped open; she slammed it shut and glared at him. "This is childish."

He hiked a brow. "You didn't deny it."

"I refuse to be baited."

"You're not denying it because you can't. That would be a lie."

"Uggg! You make me so angry."

"And you make me so happy." He stepped back and tipped his hat.

She didn't know what to say to that. It was just so...so *exasperating*. The obstinate cowboy had gotten under her skin and she just couldn't let herself falter.

No matter what her mother had tried to say to her only a few moments ago, it didn't matter.

She backed out of the parking space and caught sight of Esther Mae and Maddie in front of Heavenly Inspirations Hair Salon across the street from the feed store.

They'd had to have seen her and Treb's encounter. And there was no telling what they'd think had been going on.

# CHAPTER THIRTEEN

"**D**id y'all see that?" Norma Sue asked as she and Adela walked out of the hair salon to join Esther Mae and Maddie on the boardwalk.

"Oh, we did," Esther Mae gushed. "It was so exciting. Wasn't it, Maddie?"

"It was, actually," Maddie agreed, feeling a little as if she'd been spying but she'd been standing right in this very spot when Treb and Megan had come out of the feed store.

Norma Sue yanked her Stetson off and slapped it on her thigh. "The sparks flowing between them was like the Fourth of July. What is going on between them?"

"They looked sad," Adela said.

"I know one thing," Esther Mae snapped. "They need time together to get it straightened out."

Maddie studied the ladies as the three of them looked at one another and nodded agreement.

"They *do* for *sure,*" Norma Sue drawled, her Texas twang thick as the thoughts Maddie could practically see roaming inside that head of hers.

"Girls," Adela jumped in. "Let's go cautious here."

"Cautious." Esther Mae's green eyes flashed with excitement. "Did you see the way Megan couldn't stop looking at Treb? Oh, she'd try not to but then her gaze would go right to him and she looked like she could have drank him up like a root beer float."

"Oh my gosh." Maddie laughed, unable to stop herself. "Did you really just say that?"

Esther Mae's brow crinkled. "Have you ever had a root beer float?"

Maddie nodded, still chuckling.

"Then there you go. You know exactly how she was looking at him. Root beer floats are irresistible and you know it. Aren't they, girls?"

Norma Sue and Adela both nodded.

"She's right," the ranch woman said. "Ain't she, Adela?"

"True. Don't you agree?" The sprig of a woman beamed at her with mischief in her electric-blue eyes. "I've seen you look at Cliff that way."

"Okay, y'all have me there. Root beer float it is. So, what are y'all thinking?" Maddie couldn't help herself. No, maybe she shouldn't be encouraging the posse but she had seen the looks flashing between her friends and they did need some intervention…well, what could it hurt?

"Well," Esther Mae said, excitedly. "I think we should move over to the diner and have Sam fix us up with a root beer float and come up with a plan. What do you girls think?"

"Onward, ladies," Norma Sue commanded and Maddie fell into step with them.

There was no way she was missing out on this…

The float or the plan—not either one.

Treb had messed up. He rode his horse across the pasture in the dark, picking his way toward the thin line of light on the horizon. *What had he been thinking, pushing her like that?*

He rubbed his neck and watched the horizon inch up into a gentle pink. He halted the horse and sat frozen for a moment before he turned and headed back the way he'd come. Today, no peace had come from this outing. No solace had calmed his troubled thoughts.

Megan had a right to live her life the way she wanted to. The fact that he'd fallen for her hard and fast was a non-issue here. She had a right to her own life. And he could follow her around like a puppy dog for the rest of his life and she was in no way obligated to rethink her life decisions. No matter how much he wanted her to want him.

The truth was hard to take.

But that didn't mean it wasn't the truth. Megan

had told him from the beginning she was not marrying. That he hadn't listened was not her fault. It was his.

All his.

Megan got the call from Maddie the day after her scene with Treb in the center of town. The very idea that people had witnessed her encounter with Treb had her wanting to crawl under a stone. She knew that even if they couldn't hear the conversation, that her expression would have given away that things were tight.

The night had gone terrible. She had no emergency calls and therefore had the opportunity to sleep good—but what had she done? She'd tossed and turned and just before daylight, she'd walked out onto the porch and watched the sunrise.

Her thoughts had been on Treb as the gray hues had turned to pale pink. She thought of him riding across those dark pastures when he was troubled.

*Had he been troubled like her last night and unable to sleep?*

She almost felt as though she could feel his restless heart beating within her.

And she had the strongest urge to go to him…but of course she hadn't. She'd stayed right there on her porch and tried to make sense of the turmoil inside her.

Now, as she drove toward the part of the ranch where Maddie's orphan program was run, she fought to push him away. However, it was impossible not to think of him when she was on the ranch that he loved. Hard not to think of that night after the dance when he'd kissed her with such feeling and emotion that her world had spun. The night that she'd run like a scared rabbit and was still running.

*Love?*

Nope, she would not go there. She had work to do.

*Would Maddie ask about the scene she'd witnessed yesterday in front of Pete's? If she did, how would she answer the question?*

The minute the barn came into view, Megan saw him.

Her heart kicked with joy and then plummeted with indecision. She seesawed between the two polar opposite emotions that raced through her: to run to him or to run from him.

Treb was in the pen, bottle-feeding two newborn calves at the same time. *Where was Maddie?* Suspicion ran through Megan as she got out of the truck and walked to the fence.

*Had Treb set this up?*

"Hi. What are you doing here?" he asked, as a hungry calf tugged forcefully on the bottle.

She shifted her weight from one foot to the other and rested her casted hand on the fence before she formed an answer. "I came to check on the twins. What are you doing?"

"Maddie asked me to feed them. She didn't say anything about having called the vet."

They stared at each other across the fence.

He was so strong and masculine and yet he looked so very cute with the babies yanking and tugging at the bottles he held for them.

Yanking her gaze off him, she surveyed the calves in the other pens with their surrogate mothers. It was better to concentrate on her job than to drool over Treb.

She retrieved her bag from the truck and then unlatched the chain to enter the open pen. She could feel Treb watch her as she crossed to one of the babies that was nursing from a surrogate mother cow. The mama watched her calmly, having gotten used to Megan since her last visit. The baby wore a small cow skin over its back like a cloak. It was to fool the surrogate mother whose calf had died into believing this was her baby so that she would nurse the orphan. It was a win/win situation. A mother cow regains a calf after losing one, and a rejected or orphaned baby gained a mother to feed and protect it. The whole program touched Megan's heart.

And then there were those like the set of twins that Treb was feeding that needed to be bottle-fed because they weren't adopted, or they rebelled against a substitute.

"I love this program," she said, feeling the need to speak.

"I do too. There are a lot of cattle on the ranch that came from this program."

The baby she looked at was doing well, growing

and thriving, gaining weight and strength. She chanced a glance at Treb and stilled her heart against the thrill of watching him.

She laughed when the aggressive one butted him in the knee and then latched onto the nipple again as if it was starving. Milky slobber slung everywhere in its haste. "That one is about to tug your arm off it seems."

"Or slime me to death." Treb laughed, rich and contagious.

The look on his face and the sound of his laughter tilted her world.

He held out the bottle with the calmer calf attached. "Take this one if you want and I'll focus on Mr. Impatient here."

She stood and crossed to him. Her pulse raced as she took the bottle from him. Their fingers brushed and like always, electricity sizzled up her arm. She automatically looked to him and saw the sparkle in his blue gaze telling her that he felt it too.

She broke the connection and concentrated on the calf that hadn't let go of the bottle during the transfer.

As they stood beside each other, though she felt

the tension arcing between them, she felt mostly the enjoyment of the moment.

"I raised one of my nanny goats from a bottle. Her mother didn't make it through the birth and so I became her surrogate. She's a really good nanny goat and as sweet as pie."

"I never did get to meet your barn full of animals."

She laughed softly. "You'd like Daisy Lou. In goat years she's now as old as dirt and going to just fall over dead one day. But I'm giving her good care and a wide open pasture to live out her last days in. She's a real sweetie. And the baby goats love her. One day I got home and one was on her back."

He laughed hard. "I believe it. They can climb anything."

"Boy, that's the truth. I love to watch them. I love to watch babies, period."

"I do too." Treb looked away and Megan watched him feed the feisty calf. He was going to be a great daddy one day.

He was also going to be a great husband.

She refocused on her baby calf as it sucked the last

of the formula from the bottle. Megan tugged the bottle from its mouth and transferred the bottle to her casted hand, freeing up her right hand so she could rub the calf's forehead. "I'm going to head out. I think these little darlings are doing just fine."

"Hold on. He's through too." Treb fought the empty nipple from his calf's mouth, not an easy task. "This one is something else. I think it would eat my hand if I looked away."

"I agree. So, do you do this often?"

"Feed Maddie's babies? Yeah, whenever she asks me to. She's pretty protective of these rambunctious little ones. I'm always honored when she asks me."

He opened the fence and let her walk out before him.

Megan needed to leave but she didn't. Maybe it was because she'd had a rough night and he'd been on her mind night and day. Who was she kidding? He'd always been on her mind, from that first moment that he'd knocked on her truck window at the crack of dawn just a few short weeks ago.

"Why does she choose you?"

He shrugged. "I think it's because she found me out here one evening when I first came to the ranch."

"Really? What were you doing?"

"Just watching them." He looked almost sheepish.

"But you spend all day long with cows and calves."

"I know but...these have lost something and survived. The mom lost her baby. The baby lost its mom. And they made it together."

Megan was caught off guard by the crack in his voice and the sudden vulnerability that she sensed in him. Saw in his eyes. "You associate with them."

He nodded. "Yeah, I do. Maddie does, too, and she recognized that in me. She's like that. This program has helped her because she was abandoned as a child and this fills a gap inside her. It fills a hole in me, reminding me that life goes on after loss."

"And you're good with them." She smiled at him, feeling her heartbeat as if it were beating outside her chest.

"You are too. I enjoy seeing you with any animal you work with."

They just looked at each other for a long moment. Then he reached out and smoothed a stray hair away from her eye, moving it to her hairline and tracing his fingertips down to her jaw. A tickle of sensation traveled over her skin with his touch.

"I, um, need to go," Megan rasped, suddenly fighting tears.

She turned away. She'd left the door open and now placed her bag inside before she slid it across the seat and climbed behind the wheel.

Treb didn't make a move to stop her or talk to her again. He just lifted his hand in a good-bye and watched her leave.

She closed her eyes briefly as she drove off. Then opened them and found him still standing as still as a statue in her rearview.

It was all she could do to keep driving.

# CHAPTER FOURTEEN

Treb galloped across the field, swinging his rope in a wide loop above his head as he leaned forward and rose in the stirrups just before letting the loop sail. It rose through the air and stretched out and caught up to the steer that was headed toward the trees.

"Whew, that was some good skills you just showed off," Dalton whooped as he rode up beside Treb.

"Just doin' my job." Treb started back toward the herd. He wasn't really in the mood for conversation.

Dalton loped to catch up and had his horse fall

into step next to Treb. "Man, you need to loosen up. You're wound tighter than that rope on your saddle horn."

"Yup." There was no denying it.

"That was some great roping," Chase called as Treb reached the herd. He rode to the steer and grabbed the rope and freed the steer from the rope. It immediately rejoined the herd.

"Thanks." Treb wound his rope in and hung it on the saddle horn, ready for the next stray that tried to make a run for it.

"So did you decide to buy that place Sugar Rae showed you?" Chase asked as he loped over to join him and Dalton.

"Didn't you make the offer?" Dalton asked.

Treb had gone there yesterday after Megan had left him at the calf pens. The property had been everything he'd been hoping to find. "I did. Haven't heard back yet." He'd simply made the offer because he knew it was too good to pass up. His heart hadn't been in it, though.

"Man, you are going to have to snap out of this robot state," Rafe called from where he sat on his horse several feet away. "You're killing me. If you love this gal, then you need to not give up until you either win her over or she calls the cops."

Ty grunted from his position on the other side of Rafe. "I'm pretty sure that's called stalking and there is a law against it."

Treb frowned at them. He'd figured out that Maddie had tried to help his situation by sending Megan out to check up on her calves yesterday and he'd been aggravated about it at first. But then it had turned out to be a way for them to open up to each other a little more. It had been a good moment. Until he'd had to watch her drive away.

"The deal is," he said, "I need some kind of sign from her that she wants me around, at least a little. And I'm not getting that. I'm getting that she'd rather I just not push her."

They all looked from one another to the next and then all eyes were on him again.

"So you're giving up?" Dalton asked.

"No, I can't. She's in control, though. All I can do is wait."

Rafe cocked his head. "You've definitely got it

bad. You don't need to hang out alone tonight. You coming to Sam's for catfish with all of us tonight?"

It was fish night and everyone usually filled the diner up for Sam's fried catfish.

"I planned on going hog hunting."

Chase pinned him with sharp eyes. "If you feel the desperate need to go, then you can go after you come out with us. Rafe is right. You need friends around you right now."

"Yeah," Ty offered.

"Who knows? Maybe Megan will be there and realize she's madly in love with you." Dalton grinned at him.

"Fine. I'll be there," Treb snapped, more to get them to butt out of his love life than thinking there was even the remote possibility that Megan would declare her love for him and life would suddenly be roses and sunshine.

But it sure was a great dream.

Megan was meeting Maddie at the diner for Sam's fried catfish. Maddie had come by the clinic and personally invited her to come eat with everyone. Esther Mae had brought one of her Dorkies in for a checkup—the cross mix of Dachshund and Yorkie breed was adorable. She'd also pushed for Megan to get out and meet the town now that things were quieter and catfish night was a good place to start. Of course, the redheaded matchmaker had offered that she and Treb had looked as if they'd been having a romantic spat in town. Megan had tried really hard to get through that checkup without saying a lot.

But in the end, she had agreed that now that things were calming down she did need to start getting more involved with things other than work.

So here she was, standing out front of the diner. It might well be exactly what she needed to get her out of this funk that she was in. She pushed open the heavy swinging door and walked purposefully inside.

The room was packed. The jukebox was loud, with Wynonna Judd spilling her guts and heart all over the sound system singing "*No One Else On Earth*." Megan groaned as the lyrics basically slapped her in the face with an image of Treb.

"Megan." Maddie stood and waved her over.

Wynonna's lyrics reverberated through Megan as she weaved through the crowd. All the partners of New Horizon Ranch and their spouses were crowded around a large table, along with Treb. Of course he was here. Everyone else in town seemed to be, so why had she thought he wouldn't be? Esther Mae called her name from the table nearby where the posse sat with their spouses…all but Sam, as he and his waitresses bustled around like whirlwinds taking and delivering orders.

"You made it!" Esther Mae sang gleefully. "Y'all have fun *mingling*."

"Good company you've got there," Norma Sue called over Wynonna and then winked as if there were a log in her eye while Adela, Roy Don, and Hank all tried not to laugh.

Megan felt as though she were on a merry-go-round as Maddie grabbed her arm and yanked her to stand solidly by her side—keeping her from trying to sit anywhere but next to Treb, who just happened to be sitting next to her.

"Y'all all scooch down a little so we can get a

chair in here for Megan," Maddie directed her husband Cliff and Treb.

Megan was trapped.

Treb stood immediately and yanked his hat off. "Megan, I didn't realize you were going to be here," he said. "But I can't say I'm not happy about it." He leaned around her and tapped a cowboy on the shoulder at the table behind her and asked him whether they needed the extra chair at their table.

While he was busy acquiring her a chair, Megan gave Maddie a squinty-eyed glare and her friend giggled. *Actually giggled!*

"Sorry. I had to do it," Maddie whispered. "You'll thank me later and you know it."

"We'll see about that," Megan grunted—which only made Maddie's grin widen more.

This was twice that she'd maneuvered Megan into being around Treb. And she'd thought it was the posse she had to look out for...obviously they'd had a new member join up with them.

Treb held her chair for her and waited for her to sit in the chair he'd squeezed in beside him. True, she'd wanted to see Treb in the worst way. And now she would get to do just that, up close and personal.

"So." He leaned in after everyone greeted her. "I think we've been set up."

He was so close she could see the pale flecks of silver that dotted his blue eyes as she turned to look at him. "It appears so." The world seemed to stall as they stared at each other.

His lips lifted in a slow, sexy smile. "You sure do look pretty tonight."

*Picklefoot.* The man was not going to play fair. "Treb—"

"Megan," he broke her off with her name, sounding like a silky caress the way he said it.

Goose bumps rose across her skin and she smiled. "You aren't playing fair again."

"All's fair in love."

"Oh," she said as his gaze dropped to her lips.

Someone cleared their throat really loudly and she jumped, looking up to find a grinning Sam staring from her to Treb. A further glance revealed the entire table and a few close by were all focused on them.

"You two want catfish?" There was so much more Sam said within the context of that question and the enjoyment in his eyes.

"Yes, please," Megan blurted and then turned to face Mia and Ty, who sat across the table beside Rafe and Sadie. Dalton and Rae Anne sat at the end of the table.

"So," she said. "Did y'all order?"

Ty grinned. "We did. While you two were lost in your own little world."

And so the evening went. She and Treb were so close their arms kept rubbing during the two-hour meal. But after a while, everyone stopped teasing them and things got more comfortable as stories and conversation flowed.

Toward the end of the meal, Megan got a call from the emergency service. "I hate to leave but someone has a horse trying to colic."

She stood and so did Treb. She started to reach inside her shoulder bag for her money and he already had the money on the table.

"I've got it," he said as everyone told her good-bye.

To her surprise, he followed her out. "Mind if I come with you?"

She paused on the boarded sidewalk. "Okay, that'd be nice."

He smiled. "I was thinking the same thing."

It was a long while later when they drove away from the D Bar Ranch. The horse had lived but it had been touch-and-go there for a while. Treb was quiet as she pulled into town and parked next to his truck. At this late hour, the streets were deserted and they were all alone.

"You were amazing once again tonight," he said.

"Thank you for being there. It felt…good."

"It felt right."

His words fell between them, the truth of them bold and solid in its meaning and Megan felt them wrap around her like a hug. Like Treb's hug.

In the cab of the truck, the dashboard light cast their faces in shadows but Megan felt the gentle caress of his gaze as he reached for her. She slid from the driver's seat and met him in the middle of the bench seat as his arms wrapped around her...just like she'd waited for all evening. There was no use denying it.

Somehow Treb had eased through her defenses and she'd fallen in love with him.

"Megan, darlin', I love you. And I want to be by your side forever or as long as the good Lord gives us. And I know you might want to kick me out of the truck and lock the door but I have to lay it out here for you one more time. I'll never leave you or forsake my vows to you."

Megan couldn't breathe, couldn't speak.

"I'm askin' for your hand and your heart in marriage."

She'd fought this. Believed she couldn't give her heart and her control of her life over to a man. But in the end, she'd realized that without Treb none of that mattered. She wanted and trusted him.

"Do you love me, Megan? I'm in love with you and everything about you and your life."

She cupped his face with hers. "I do. And it turns

out I'm yours and that makes me happy. We fit."

His smile lit the truck. "That's what I want to hear." And then he pulled her close and covered her lips with his. It was perfect...the perfect start of their life together.

And that thought filled Megan with joy and wiped all her fears away.

Excerpt from

# MADDIE'S SECRET BABY

New Horizon Ranch, Book Seven

# CHAPTER ONE

With her mug of coffee in hand, Maddie Masterson walked outside and leaned against the porch railing. The early morning view of her cowboy riding his horse was a beautiful sight...with the rosy pink and melon sunrise glowing behind him— it was an awe inspiring sight.

It just didn't get any better than that.

For a girl who'd had no one in her life to love until

Cliff Masterson swept into her world, the sight of him always sent her heart thumping and joy cascading through her. Even after almost a year of marriage.

She sighed and murmured, "Yes ma'am, you are officially a sap over him." She sipped her coffee as peace flowed through her.

She was so blessed...

And late.

Spinning away, she hurried inside to dress for the day in tank top, jeans boots and a ponytail topped with a straw Stetson...her cowgirl uniform. She loved her life.

Her thoughts went back to Cliff and the life they were building together. She'd never forget that first day she'd met him, when he'd jumped between her and an angry bull and saved her from getting trampled.

Sparks had flown because, despite him saving her, they'd managed to get off on the wrong foot, locking horns right from the get go.

Like flint on rock went together, so did they. Goodness, they'd made sparks.

And nothing had changed about that.

They still could. Oh yes indeed, they could.

Rushing back into the kitchen, she grabbed an insulted coffee mug and filled it to the brim, then hurried back onto the porch. The sun was up now, soft and gentle, a tease before it rose to its full fury later that afternoon. It was going to be a scorcher.

"Mornin' gorgeous," Cliff called as he locked the gate and strode toward her across the yard.

Their gazes locked, and even from a hundred yards, Maddie's pulse jumped and her insides melted like butter.

He raised a hand in an easy wave. "You *sure* do look pretty in the morning light, Mrs. Masterson."

She laughed. "Now I know you're blinded by love. I'm about as plain as they come."

"Your hair could be a mess, and you could be covered in dirt," he drawled. "But darlin', you'd still be beautiful to me."

There went that melting heart again.

He made her feel beautiful no matter what she looked like. Even when she came in hot, sweaty and covered in grime after a day working cattle, he could look at her, and she felt beautiful.

"I think you're pretty, too," she teased. Her husband was one handsome, rugged male, and pretty was not a word to describe him. What that man did for a pair of chaps and a cowboy hat never ceased to amaze her.

His eyes narrowed. "You know those are fighting words."

"Oh yeah? What'ch gonna do about it?"

He smiled that crooked smile and didn't even pause as he stepped onto the porch and swept her into his arms. "Love you forever. Good morning, Mrs. Masterson," he said, then covered her mouth with his.

Maddie sighed and wrapped her arms around him and hung on. She sank into his strong arms, feeling happier and more female and desirable than she'd ever thought possible. Being a woman in a man's world wasn't easy. She wrangled cattle, used branding irons, dug post holes and built fence, among a host of other ranching jobs, so it took a lot to make her feel feminine.

Cliff Masterson had made her feel that way from

the first moment they'd met.

Now Maddie's arms tightened around his neck, and she counted her blessings. This was where she was born to be, with this man forever. He kissed with a gentle yet powerful certainty that melted her insides and heated her blood. It was certainly a jumpstart to a day that gallons of caffeine could not compete with. Nothing could.

By the time he lifted his head, she could no longer think straight.

His eyes were warm as he smiled a lazy smile, straightened his hat and studied her. "It's probably a good thing you work on one ranch and I work on ours, because I might not ever get anything done. Kissing you is just too enjoyable. And more tempting than a dip in a cool creek on a hot summers day."

She chuckled. "I agree. I'm pretty partial to it."

He studied her, then suddenly his brows dipped and his gaze sharpened. "Are you feeling okay? You're pale."

"Pale? Are you kidding?" She tugged her hat off and fanned herself. "I'm probably red as a firetruck after that kiss."

He shook his head. "Nope. Pale as a piece of bread."

"You certainly know how to douse a fire. I'll admit I'm a little tired, but it's not a big deal. I haven't been sleeping well."

"Why?"

She shrugged. "I don't know. I'll get some rest tonight. For now, I have to run. Your brother and the others are going to start thinking I'm slacking if I don't hurry."

He laughed. "Yeah, right. You know that's not true." He gave her a quick kiss on the lips and let her go. "Tonight you're getting some sleep. You've got circles under your eyes."

"Gee, thanks, buster." She glanced over her shoulder and smiled. It was nice to have someone in her life who worried about her. Until Cliff, she'd never had that.

He frowned. "I'm serious, babe. Maybe you need to take a day off. You work harder than any woman I know. You can take a day off."

"I'm fine." She climbed into her truck. "I love you and good luck. Hope you sell the horse. And drive safe delivering your bulls to the rodeo."

"Thanks. I feel good about it. I'll be on the road by noon to deliver the bulls, and if my schedule goes as planned, I'll be back here by six to fix you dinner. You can at least rest then."

She hung her head out the open window. "Thanks. We can celebrate your horse sale."

"Sounds like a plan to me." He lifted his hand in goodbye as she left.

Excitement filled her as she headed down the drive. This sale would be a lot to celebrate. Rodeo bookings for his rodeo bulls had been strong, and the cutting horse business was looking good too. The ranch might be in the black in the first year of business. She was proud for Cliff. Leaving the competitive world of bull riding at the prime of his career had been hard on him, but he'd been ready to start the next chapter of his life. She wanted this to work out for him. For them.

She couldn't wait to celebrate.

That new chapter of his life had included her and his hope--*their* hope--of a family. As she drove away, her thoughts went to another celebration she really wanted to experience with her amazing husband...having a baby.

Oh how she wanted a baby.

With Mother's Day approaching, a child of their own was heavy on her heart and mind. Growing their family weighed heavy on both of them. Every time they celebrated anything, they were also working on making their baby dream come true.

That was a win/win situation if ever there was one.

Her mouth went dry suddenly, and she felt a wave of weakness wash over her.

She'd ignored the feeling earlier, but now she acknowledged that she didn't feel exactly well. She'd been really tired the last few days, drug out with just no energy. And she'd been getting a little queasy off and on too. For a girl who was hardly ever ill, it had been an odd feeling that she'd pushed through. She didn't have time or temperament to be ill, but—

An exciting idea hit Maddie, and she straightened in the seat. Her hands gripped the steering wheel in a stranglehold. Was it possible?

Could she be pregnant?

# More Books in the Series

## New Horizon Ranch Series

Her Texas Cowboy: Cliff (Book 1)

Rescued by Her Cowboy: Rafe (Book 2)

Protected by Her Cowboy: Chase (Book 3)

Loving Her Best Friend Cowboy: Ty (Book 4)

Family for a Cowboy: Dalton (Book 5)

The Mission of Her Cowboy: Treb (Book 6)

Maddie's Secret Baby: Short Story (Book 7)

This Cowgirl Loves This Cowboy: Austin (Book 8)

## Check out Debra's Other Series

Star Gazer Inn of Corpus Christi Bay

Cowboys of Dew Drop, Texas

Cowboys of Ransom Creek

Sunset Bay Romance

Texas Brides & Bachelors

Turner Creek Ranch Series

Texas Matchmaker Series

Windswept Bay Series

# About the Author

Debra Clopton is a USA Today bestselling & International bestselling author who has sold over 3.5 million books. She has published over 81 books under her name and her pen name of Hope Moore.

Under both names she writes clean & wholesome and inspirational, small town romances, especially with cowboys but also loves to sweep readers away with romances set on beautiful beaches surrounded by topaz water and romantic sunsets.

Her books now sell worldwide and are regulars on the Bestseller list in the United States and around the world. Debra is a multiple award-winning author, but of all her awards, it is her reader's praise she values most. If she can make someone smile and forget their worries for a few hours (or days when binge reading one of her series) then she's done her job and her heart is happy. She really loves hearing she kept a reader from doing the dishes or sleeping!

A sixth-generation Texan, Debra lives on a ranch in Texas with her husband surrounded by cattle, deer, very busy squirrels and hole digging wild hogs. She enjoys traveling and spending time with her family.

Visit Debra's website and sign up for her newsletter for updates at: www.debraclopton.com

Check out her Facebook at: www.facebook.com/debra.clopton.5

Follow her on Instagram at: debraclopton_author

or contact her at debraclopton@ymail.com

Made in United States
North Haven, CT
19 March 2023

34269132R00117